America's Social Democratic Future

W. E. Smith

Also by W. E. Smith

Novels
Tanaki on the Shore
Ver Sacrum
Bal Harbour
I've Got a Right to Sing the Blues
Wolftamer

Short Stories
I Wanna Hear It Again
He on Honeydew Hath Fed

The United States is great because its people are good; if the people of the United States ever cease to be good, the United States will cease to be great

Congressman James Clyburn to the South Carolina Democratic Party, January, 2024 (often attributed to Alexis de Toqueville)

Acknowledgement

The author wishes to thank Daniel Gross, PhD, and Henry Smith, JD, for their astute comments on the manuscript-in-production

American's Social Democratic Future

America's Social Democratic Future: Preface

The citizens of the United States find ourselves, at this writing, at a signal juncture. While American political history has for several generations vacillated between right and left, between conservative and liberal, between Republicans and Democrats, there is a sense today that the gulf that separates the two poles of American political discourse is wider than ever. I believe I am not alone in feeling that the nation's psyche is undergoing a profound change, instigated not only by the recent pandemic but also by a new generation with decreasing tolerance for racism, sexism and the marginalization of any group that finds itself outside the rails of social norms; by the tragically mean-spirited Trump presidency (aided and abetted by a morally bankrupt Republican congressional delegation); by the ravages of globalization, with its decades-long transition to a service economy and concomitant hollowing out of the middle class (trends exacerbated by successful Republican attacks on worker representation); and by the existential threat of environmental degradation and global warming. As a result of these converging factors, it feels that we are straining as we have not done since the 1960s toward new formulas and a revised social contract.

The purpose of this small volume is to present a vision of a new American future, one built around the core concepts of *social democracy*. It is the author's conviction that *social democracy* is the far-and-away winner of any comparison between available concepts for the social, economic and political organization of complex modern societies. Those countries best known for practicing social democracy—such as Norway, Denmark and the Netherlands—consistently top rankings of citizen happiness and well-being. While not in itself disposi-tive, this is a good advertisement for this mode of social or-ganization. In the following pages, I will present a detailed case for why the core tenets and practices of social democracy offer the best way forward for the United States. Some of the proposals I offer may seem radical to the reader, and I do not believe that each aspect of the vision I will lay out in the coming pages is likely to gain political acceptance in the immediate or even near future.[1] What I aim to present here is instead a destination worthy of setting our sights on, along with a set of principles which will guide our journey. We might say that the book is more a desideratum than a set of practical policy recommendations: and after all, we are awash in the latter, but sorely lacking in commonly held visions. I write from the standpoint not of an economist or social scientist but a moral philosopher in the tradition of Henry Moore, Voltaire, or John Stuart Mill.

Like all social democrats, I consider myself a person of the Left, but what we might call "the Left" is in America today a luxuriant garden, teeming with all manner of both standard and exotic flower and foliage. As the Left's sole effective standard bearer in the United States, the Democratic Party is celebrated as a "big tent," capable of accommodating disparate and even contradictory elements. While some believe that this approach allows the Party to assemble the largest possible coalition, it also leads to ideological incoherence as well as operational difficulties: witness the intra-party feud that nearly derailed passage of President Biden's "roads and bridges" infrastructure legislation and left his other major legislative package, the so-called "social infrastructure" bill, indefinitely stalled, with "progressives" and "centrists" squared off against one another, each with their red lines and ultimatums.

Some dissension among the Left is of course natural, normal, inevitable and healthy. In European parliamentary

---

1. For a detailed, comprehensive treatment of practical policy proposals for the here and now, building on already existing programs, see scholar Lane Kenworthy's invaluable *Social Democratic Capitalism* (2021).

democracies, the Left is typically fractured into several parties running the gamut from communists to centrists. Ideological differences between these parties are clearly articulated and coalitions formed, when necessary, based on explicitly stated compromises between competing positions and programs. In our American system, where the two major parties must bear the entire load of political ideas and ideals, such jockeying takes place within the unitary Democratic and Republican parties. The Republican Party has done a good job of defining itself: it is against government regulation and taxes and opposed to any changes to American culture of the 1950s. The Democrats have not done so well in this respect. We have center-leftists who applaud our free-enterprise system (the majority of the party) as well as vague denunciations of "capitalism" with equally vague praise of "socialism" coming from the left wing. The Party attempts to stay ahead of the curve on evolving culture-war and identity politics issues, beholden to disparate grievance groups for its tenuous majority, often at the expense of alienating the broad middle-ground of American society. In this two-party system, it is incumbent upon the Democratic Party, as the Left's sole standard-bearer, to capture the largest share of voters possible. This will require a level of ideological coherence that will allow the average voter to understand exactly what the Party stands for over time. We cannot afford to allow those espousing minoritarian positions important to only fringe areas of the Left to capture the media spotlight. In our age of infotainment and "gotcha" sound-bite political discourse, the most outrageous comments will receive the most attention, regardless of the extent to which they represent the Party as a whole. Fringe ideas will then be weaponized by the Right, branding the entire Party with positions which can lead to disaster at the polls.

However some may celebrate the Democrat Party's big tent, we of the Left must recognize that, if we are not completely losing (as of this writing), we are certainly not *winning*. The Democratic Party's razor-thin margins in the 117th Congress left little room for maneuver in passing federal legislation, with Republican filibuster looming over nearly every initiative, and in the 2022 mid-term elections the Party lost even this precarious control. At the level of state assemblies, which control many of the most vital aspects of our lives (policing, education, public health) things are even bleaker. The 2022 elections left Republicans in control of both legislative chambers in 28 states, with Democrats controlling both chambers in only 19, and the two major parties splitting control in the remaining 3 states. At the executive level, Republicans occupy the governor's mansion in 26 states, with Democrats in only 24. Republicans control both legislative houses along with the governor's mansion in 22 states (a "trifecta"), Democrats in only 17. Down ballot ticket-splitting (with Biden at the top and Republicans below) in 2020, as well as polling, suggest that many Biden votes were votes *against* Donald Trump, not votes *for* the Democratic brand. A recent poll, in fact, suggests that even Democratic voters have no clear idea of what the Democratic Party stands for.[2]

The American Left's lack of ideological coherence is costing us dearly. It is now accepted by most objective observers that third party voters, Bernie Sanders abstainers and party-switchers brought Donald Trump to power, with all the damage which has resulted: most saliently, hundreds of thousands of needless Covid deaths and a reactionary Supreme Court we will likely have to live with for decades to come. Perhaps this could have been avoided were Democrats able to articulate a common program which could convince substantial majorities of voters to back the Party at the polls.

A crucial goal of this volume, one to which we will turn presently, is to distinguish social democracy, as the term is used by this author, from other strains active on the modern American Left. I will clarify a coherent ideology of social organization and provide a set of terms and concepts with which to speak about social democratic ideals, beginning with the

2. See https://www.politico.com/news/2021/11/23/
dems-joe-biden-infrastructure-midterms-523194

concept of "social democracy" itself. I think the reader will see that in truth, most Americans on the left, whether they currently call themselves "liberals," "progressives," "Democrats" or even "socialists," are in fact already social democrats. If we can understand that fact, we can embrace a social democratic vision across the American Left and, speaking with one voice, convince a working majority of the American public to back our programs.

Part I

Defining Social Democracy

Defining Social Democracy:

What Social Democracy Is Not

Social Democracy Is Not "Socialism" (and Why I Argue for a Social Democratic, Not a "Socialist," Future) . . .

Speaking in a debate during his first candidacy for the presidency, self-proclaimed socialist Bernie Sanders suggested that the "socialism" he propounded was nothing other than the kind of government successfully practiced in the Scandinavian nations of Denmark, Sweden and Norway. Not long afterward, while delivering a keynote lecture at Harvard's Kennedy School of Government, Danish Prime Minister Lars Løkke Rasmussen, who might be presumed to know something about the matter, felt compelled to correct the champion of the Democratic Socialists of America: "I know that some people in the U.S. associate the Nordic model with some sort of socialism," Rasmussen said. "Therefore I would like to make one thing clear. Denmark is far from a socialist planned economy. Denmark is a market economy." Rasmussen explained further that "the Nordic model is an expanded welfare state which provides a high level of security for its citizens, but it is also a successful market economy with much freedom to pursue your dreams and live your life as you wish."

This anecdote sums up as well as anything the confusion that has reigned for the last dozen years over the American Left about the term "socialism." Especially during the run-up to the 2016 elections, spurred largely by Sanders' embrace of the term, newspapers and magazines were flush with articles telling us that the current generation of young people were far more favorable to "socialism" than elders whose ideas about the topic were supposedly shaped by the ideological battles of the Cold War. When one looked under the hood of these claims, however, what one found was that respondents to polls asking about socialism did not seem to have any very clear idea—and certainly no shared idea—about what "socialism" was. What was typically found was that respondents to these polls, like Bernie Sanders himself, tended to conflate "socialism" with Scandinavian and other European countries characterized by fulsome social safety nets. Knowledgeable political scientists and economists valiantly fielded articles attempting to set the record straight, explaining that the Scandinavian nations practiced not "socialism" but "social democracy." But breathless journalists, eager for any promising click-bait, continued to talk about the growing appeal of "socialism."

So what is "socialism," and why am I so keen to distinguish it from "social democracy?" First, let me state that it is possible to find differing definitions of "socialism." The current Wikipedia article describes a couple dozen varieties, from "Marxist-Leninism" and "Stalinism" to "market socialism," "anarcho-communism" and even "Buddhist socialism." But we need not get lost in the jungle of these conceptions, few of them exemplified by any real-world experience, in order to constructively use the term "socialism." For at heart, all varieties of socialism, if the term is to mean anything useful, are based on the idea of collective control and/or ownership of the "means of production." Here is the dictionary definition of *socialism* (*Merriam Webster's 11th Collegiate Edition*):

> *1. Any of various economic and political theories advocating collective or governmental ownership and administration of the means of production and distribution of goods.*
> *2.a. A system of society or group living in which there is no private property;*
> *b. a system or condition of society in which the means of production are owned and controlled by the state.*

You get the idea. Think, for example, the "Union of Soviet *Socialist* Republics." True socialists believe, in general, that the state (or the "collective") should own all property and control all economic activity. Traditional socialists believe that allowing private citizens to amass *capital* (money, property, machinery) in order to engage in economic activity (factories, stores, construction), hiring others to work in these enterprises and retaining proceeds above expenses as *profit*, is inherently unjust and even immoral ("exploitation"). It is true that some self-defined socialists of modern America will tell you that they do not propose putting *all* economic activity in the hands of the state, only major sectors like transportation and steel production. Such proponents alter the classic definition of "socialism," creating a hybrid socialist/private-enterprise system which I believe would be more effective than a purely socialist system but still not as efficient as a mainly private-enterprise system.[1]

Other self-proclaimed socialists will say that they do not wish the state, *per se*, to take over economic activity, but that economic enterprises (i.e., businesses) should be owned and run by the people who work in them (collective ownership). My argument against this proposal is two-fold. First, it ignores how business enterprises get started in the first place—by *entrepreneurs*. Proponents of this strain of socialism seem to believe that after an entrepreneur goes through the struggle to create an enterprise, the state will come in and take away the enterprise in order to place it in the hands of its employees. The likely result of this strategy, it would seem obvious, would be that you would soon have no more entrepreneurs; for who would go through the stress, strain and hard work to create a business from scratch if one knew that, once it were up and running, it would be taken away? My second argument against

---

1. In regard to the term "socialist," one should not be misled by the many European political parties which carry the word "socialist" in their name (France's *Parti socialiste*, Spain's *Partido Socialista Obrero Español*, Portugal's *Partido Socialista*). When social democracy initially emerged in the early 20th Century, it was conceived of as a station along the way to a fully "socialist" (i.e., "communist") society, a goal which the socialist left felt to be impractical at that time. Over the decades from the 1940s through the 90s, these "socialist" parties divested themselves of the goal of achieving true "socialism" and now regard social democracy as an end in itself.

this version of socialism is that no change in our laws or institutions is required to implement it. If a group of workers—say, the mechanics in a garage—want to have their own enterprise, they are already empowered to create it. They merely need pool their resources (scrimp, save and take out loans, as most entrepreneurs do), jointly acquire the necessary resources (shop, machinery) and run the business themselves. This is merely a *partnership*, an already well-established legal entity. Why isn't this done more often, you might ask, since it is perfectly possible today? The reason is, I believe, that most employees do not have a calling to be *entrepreneurs*. Entrepreneurs are a form of leader, and not everyone is a leader, just as not everyone is a musician, a skilled woodworker—or a talented mechanic. In private enterprise systems the collective citizenry of a nation makes a deal with potential entrepreneurs. In exchange for their vision and leadership abilities, society allows them a fairly free hand to start and control economic enterprises. These entrepreneurs' role in private enterprise economies will be developed further just ahead, but for now I will simply emphasize that, even taking non-standard definitions such as "collective ownership" into account, socialists do not believe that private individuals should be able to amass capital ("capitalism") and hire their fellow citizens for economic enterprises, keeping proceeds above expenses as their personal income.

Social democrats, in contrast to socialists, have no problem with *capitalism*—with allowing private citizens to amass *capital* (property, machinery, raw materials) and, using that capital, to organize economic enterprises which they will then *own*. However, let me say at this juncture that *capitalism* has become such a loaded term, often conflated with *laissez-faire* (unregulated) capitalism, that I find it more useful to employ the term "private enterprise economy." This is the term that I will generally use throughout this volume.[2]

2. Merriam Webster's defines capitalism as follows: "an economic system characterized by private or corporate ownership of capital goods, by investments that are determined by private decision, and by prices,

A longstanding argument against socialism has been that such systems are not as economically efficient or productive as private enterprise economies. The U.S.S.R. and other nations of the ex-Soviet Block were notorious for both a paucity and lack of variety in consumer goods, for multiple families sharing single apartments, for long lines to purchase scarce items which were readily at hand for citizens of capitalist economies (an orange, for example) and for reduced technological innovation. It has been the opinion of most informed observers that in removing the possibility of entrepreneurship—by making it impossible for a citizen to achieve more by taking the initiative to lead, or by working harder and smarter—socialist regimes destroy the incentive for citizens to excel in the economic sphere. As the old Soviet workers' joke had it, "They pretend to pay us, and we pretend to work."

The socialist model is a top-down one. Since the state owns everything and controls all economic production, decisions about what is produced and how it is distributed are made by political actors and bureaucrats. In a private-enterprise economy, by contrast, each and every citizen has the right to create an economic enterprise: a local pizza shop, a line of clothing, a tire factory. In a socialist economy the bureaucrats who make decisions about production and distribution must attempt to determine, from their perches atop society, what is needed in each community and in each sector. In a private enterprise economy, local actors, intimately familiar with their own communities and neighbors, are much better situated to determine whether, for example, a new bakery might be welcomed in town (or, just as likely, a Dunkin' Donuts franchise). Similarly, a logistics manager, after working for a trucking company for ten years, will be ideally placed to determine if the local and sectoral marketplace is in need of another transport company. In addition, she will understand precisely how that marketplace works and how such a company might be organized.

---

production, and the distribution of goods that are determined mainly by competition in a free market."

Private enterprise economies unleash the economic creativity of every potential entrepreneur. In this "bottom-up" approach, the power to create the framework of our communities' and nation's economic life is distributed laterally throughout society. Such a system allows natural leaders to self-select. Those with an inspired vision of an economic enterprise that will benefit the lives of their fellow citizens are free, if their instinct is true, and if they can gather the necessary resources and organize the enterprise effectively, to make that vision a reality.

Such self-selecting economic leaders are held to account by a very strict supervisor: the marketplace. If they miscalculate—if there is not a sufficient market for the business they create; if they do not organize it efficiently; if the business does not answer to the needs and desires of their fellow citizens—the enterprise will not endure, and the would-be entrepreneur likely face considerable personal disruption and hardship. Many argue for socialism on the grounds that market economies are undemocratic. But, in fact, market economies are democratic in the extreme. Every day American consumers spend billions of pennies for goods and services, and each penny spent is a vote for what kinds of products and services will be offered. Those business creators who receive plenty of votes, in the form of pennies, will see their enterprises endure and grow. The enterprises of those business creators who receive an inadequate number of penny-votes will not survive. The American public, through these purchases, freely and sovereignly determines what products and services will be offered. Such a system is incredibly subtle in its operations—down to the level of the penny, to be more precise. It is far more democratic, being responsive to a minutely gradated continuum of needs and desires, than the process by which we elect political leaders, for example. And since consumers shop not only for function but also for taste and customer service, each penny shifted from one enterprise to another subtly alters, along with the range of goods and services on offer, the customer-relations practices of businesses (who must respond to consumers' wishes if they are to survive).

That "top-down" socialist economies, with decisions about the production and delivery of goods and services made by state bureaucrats, have never been able to provide the quantity and range of goods produced by private enterprise economies, nor been able to satisfy the material needs and desires of their citizens as well as private enterprise economies, is not surprising. How could a state agency tasked with, say, the production of footwear, possibly react as nimbly to consumer wishes as a large assortment of private companies, each embedded in the marketplace and each kept on its toes (sorry) by the need to amass enough votes in the form of pennies to stay afloat? It was traditionally joked about classic socialist economies like the Soviet Union and its satellites that consumers did in fact have a choice: to use the example of shoes, a choice between brown or black, all of exactly the same style. While this is surely an exaggeration, it encapsulates a truth about the difference between top-down, socialist economies and bottom-up, private enterprise economies.

Thus, a private enterprise economy allows for an economy that is far more responsive to the material needs and desires of consumer-citizens. But man does not live by bread alone, and it is my conviction that a private enterprise economy also affords its members several non-material advantages over a socialist system. First, private enterprise economies allow for more personal freedom than a socialist system, offering every citizen the opportunity to become an economic leader, following their particular destinies and pursuing their potentials. Second, private economies, by fostering individual initiative, provide far greater richness in cultural and intellectual life. Great accomplishments in the arts and sciences generally come from inspired individuals, not through government committees. Lastly, I believe that a private-enterprise economy best answers to our spiritual health. A private-enterprise economy requires would-be economic leaders, as we have seen, to devise and execute a plan for an economic enterprise that must receive adequate penny-votes to pay for the business's overhead, including the salaries of the company's employees, while leaving enough extra to support the entrepreneur (and pay back initial investments). In order for the business to survive, the original business plan as well as its execution must satisfy the needs and desires of the entrepreneur's neighbors and fellow citizens. This being the case, private enterprise economies force would-be economic leaders to carefully ponder the needs and desires of their neighbors, both initially and continually, for only those entrepreneurs who provide a real benefit to their customers (as determined by the customers themselves, in the form of penny-votes) will endure as economic leaders. By a similar logic, salaried employees must see themselves, on some level, as entrepreneurs, for they must offer value-added to enterprises in which they hope to participate. In this way the system exerts a constant pressure upon each of us to determine where our best talents lie, and to identify and develop those potentials that might benefit our communities. This, for me, is the essence of a spiritual life: to find one's best way to be of use to others. In a sense, a private-enterprise system forces each of us, if we are to make a living, to sublimate our tendencies toward selfishness at least enough to find some way in which we can be useful to society. By contrast, state-run businesses in socialist economies have been notorious not only for a paucity of choice and availability of goods, but also surly and arrogant service, for the government functionaries in charge need not answer to the consumer.

Individuals as well as the larger society benefit in a private enterprise system, because each of us is given wide latitude to follow a dream which we feel might be of use to others. A young dress designer, full of talent and certain of her vision, can start her own line; the buying public will determine whether she has aimed rightly. The designer is granted the ability to fully develop her potential; the rest of us stand to benefit by her talent, vision and courage. It is hard to imagine how such things can work in a society in which the state makes all decisions. Bureaucrats are necessary and do many things well. Ground-breaking innovation and creativity are not typically among them.

Before leaving the topic, I will advance one final argument against socialism (the ownership and control of the "means of production" by the state). I, like most on the Left, believe that too-great concentrations of economic power—monopolies—are not a good thing. In fact, I know of no one calling for "socialism" who does not claim to share this sentiment. I cannot understand, therefore, why a self-avowed socialist would consider placing *all* economic activity in the hands of a single actor: the state. If the state could ever be made as responsive to the citizenry as business enterprises are to the marketplace, such a system might be worth considering. But it is the very competition among business actors, each vying for consumers' penny-votes, that forces enterprises to produce goods and services that consumers want and need and to deliver them in a manner consistent with consumers' wishes. Where the state owns and controls all economic enterprise, there is no recourse for citizen-consumers who are not happy with what it offers. They cannot "take their business elsewhere," because there is no "elsewhere" in such regimes. There is no mechanism for keeping producers honest. This explains the relative deprivation of those who lived under the Soviet system, the poverty of Cubans, the tragedy of scarcity in Venezuela today, and the corruption which never fails to saturate all such regimes.

In brief the state, with its cumbersome bureaucracies, can never compete with the responsiveness of millions of transactions percolating through the economy every day, where consumers are constantly placing their penny-votes in the marketplace. There is a built-in unworkability to the socialist idea. This is why, I believe, such a system has never been installed and maintained under a democratic political regime. Where democracy is allowed, citizens will eventually grow tired of this unworkable ideal and reinstate a private enterprise economy—as we have seen happen in the satellite states of the former Soviet Union. We also see, in states that were first democratic and then installed some version of socialism—Venezuela, for example—that the state must progressively destroy democracy if it attempts to stay the course with the unworkable socialist model. With democracy in tact, the citizenry will not long tolerate the continuation of this failed experiment.

Now that I have praised the private enterprise economic model, a couple of caveats are in order. First, though we social democrats believe in an essentially private-enterprise economy, that is not to say that there might never arise circumstances which justify government ownership, or shares of ownership, in certain sectors, for example when Sweden temporarily nationalized its ailing banks in the 1990s. Government control, whole or partial, can also be justified for certain services which require monolopy ownership, for example, the postal service. Second, nothing written here should be taken to mean that the private enterprise system (*capitalism*, if you wish) practiced in the United States today is without flaws or beyond improvement. I believe in fact that the economic system practiced in the United States today is fraught with injustice, inefficiency and illogic. I do not believe, however, that the problem is with a private enterprise system (*capitalism*) per se. So while, in the following pages, I will address many respects in which I believe our current socio-economic system should be altered, I will not argue for state or collective control of the means of production. Finally, although I argue for private enterprise and against state control of the means of production, I believe in a fulsome and unapologetic role for the state in regulating the private business enterprises which social democracy celebrates. In my social democratic vision the democratic collective, operating through the state, has plenipotentiary, or complete, authority. The ownership of capital by an entrepreneur is therefore never absolute. The democratically elected state may tax such property at whatever level it deems necessary and just; it may determine the manners in which that property can or cannot be used; and it may impose any regulations, including those affecting employees' pay or working conditions, which it deems suitable. These ideas will be developed in depth in later chapters, but suffice here to say that entrepreneurs under these conditions are not free-market mavericks unbound by any rules except the logic of the marketplace. They are more akin to concessionaires who have been granted the means to carry out certain functions for the benefit of all.

Social Democracy is Not Identity Politics — and Why I Argue Against an Identity Politics Future . . .

Another active strain on the American left today is identity politics. I define identity politics as a political dynamic in which a citizen of a nation, state or community primarily identifies not with the nation, state or community as a whole but with a subset of that nations' citizens. In the United States today the largest subsets with which some citizens identify are women, Americans racialized as "Black," and Americans racialized as "Latino."[3] For those who operate

3. America's social and culturally constructed concepts of "race" are inconsistent and illogical. What's worse, the terminologies we use to describe the made-up concept of "race" tend to make things worse, not better. In those American states that sanctioned slavery and discrimination against people with African ancestry, the test as to whether a person fit into this persecuted cohort was "one drop of blood." That is, the suspected presence of a single ancestor from Africa, even if all other ancestors were of non-African ancestry, would result in the application of the racialized category "negro" and with this, the deprivation of equal rights. And we have carried this logic forward into the present day. Note, for example, that Barack Obama, though of exactly 50% European and 50% African ancestry, is considered "Black." In general terms, a majority of Americans generally racialized as "Black" have some degree of European ancestry. Likewise, members of the racialized categories "Latinos," "Asian Americans"

from the identity politics mindset, views on public policy

---

and "Native Americans" (applied both by self and others) often have significant European ancestry (almost all "Latinos," for example, are what in Latin America is called *mestizo*, a mixed genetic heritage of pre-Columbian peoples and Spanish conquerors; the U.S. Census treats Latinos as a branch of some other "racial category," with the possibility to check one's "ethnicity" as "Hispanic or Latino" or "non-Hispanic or Latino"). As to those people racialized as "White," DNA testing has revealed that a significant percentage of these Americans, particularly those from former slave states, not infrequently derive not insignificant percentages of their DNA from African ancestors. I find the terms "Black" and "White" to be not only inaccurate—I have met few Americans whose skin is either black or white (mine, for example, is tan, which is a shade of brown, as is the skin of most people I know who are racialized as "Black")—but also seemingly designed to portray people with any degree of African ancestry as the polar opposite of people who appear to be of predominantly European ancestry. After all, what could be more different than "black" and "white?" Why adopt this falsified view of the situation, when in reality almost all of us are varying shades of brown? I am tempted to ask who is vested in maintaining the fiction that we are somehow diametrically distinct from those whose skin is a lighter or a darker shade of brown than ours? Nor am I a fan of the term "people of color." First, in regard to being, myself, a person racialized as "White," and therefore not among the "people of color," my response is, "Wait, but I do have a color, a sort of reddish-gold tan." Further, this phrase implies that there is some good reason why those who are not racialized as "White" should all be lumped together in opposition to those racialized as "White." It implies, further, that those not racialized as "White" share common interests. However, recent court cases which feature Americans racialized as "Asian" suing colleges to stop affirmative action programs designed to favor Americans racialized as "Black," or the recent spate of hate-motivated attacks against Americans racialized as "Asian" by people racialized as "Black," would seem to indicate otherwise, as would the growing diversity in political affiliations among Americans racialized as both "Black" and "Latino" (significant percentages of voters in both categories voted for Donald Trump in 2020). For these reasons, in this volume I will refer to our racialized groups as "Americans racialized as black (ARB)," Americans racialized as White" (ARW), "Americans racialized as Latino" (ARL) and so on.

and political priorities are shaped largely if not chiefly by the sentiment of being part of a subset of the body politic with interests and goals different—and often at odds with—the interests and goals of those outside one's subset. (Note, in this context, that Black Lives Matter has made no protest when individuals other than Americans racialized as "black" (ARBs) were killed by police—a majority of police killings—even when circumstances were egregiously unjustified.)

A corollary of the identity politics dynamic is that individuals claiming to speak for various identity segments make claims upon the state for special considerations for their sub-group. More specifically, identity politics spokespeople (*self-declared* spokespeople, for none of our identity groups hold elections to choose spokespeople) claim that their group has suffered and continues to suffer injustice at the hands of American society. For the extreme practitioner of identity politics, rectification of the wrongs they feel their identity group is currently experiencing, along with retribution for wrongs suffered previously, is the primary political motivator and the lens through which all other social and political questions are viewed.

I believe there is a great deal of truth in many of the claims made by self-identified spokespeople for various identity groups. The central claim of the major identity groups—that heterosexual males of mainly European ancestry have traditionally enjoyed a right to more power and influence than those who are not heterosexual male and of European ancestry—is indisputable. I can not look benignly, however, upon the idea of an America composed of competing tribalisms each of whose chief aim is to get what is theirs as against other groups. ARBs (Americans racialized as "Black") and ARLs (Americans racialized as "Latino") and women are only the most populous of these groups. There of course are others—Americans racialized as Asian (ARA), Muslims and many more. And as was inevitably to occur, we now have the resurgence of Americans racialized as "White" organizing to make sure that their racialized group doesn't get left out of the scramble for tribal power, influence and prosperity. I suspect that those who would wish this kind of future on America were either not alive at the time, or have forgotten the cases, of Rwanda or the former Yugoslavia.

Things could get very ugly.

Tribalism is very old in the human genome. The impulse to make snap judgments about whether a newly encountered *homo sapiens* is friend or foe, based on immediately perceivable outward characteristics, may have been adaptive to wandering prehistoric bands competing for resources and territory. But in a modern, multi-cultural society such impulses are counter-productive. For this reason, we must remain vigilant to continually counter the lazy impulse to assume that because someone looks different than you (or speaks differently, or dresses differently) they *are* different. Brown, black, and white horses do not divide themselves into different sections of a pasture. *They* are smart enough to know that they are all *horses*. And it is not only Americans racialized as "White" who harbor racist thoughts and feelings.

Numerous studies have found racism toward other groups among Americans racialized as "Black," "Latino," "Asian," "Native American" and all other racialized categories. A significant proportion of pandemic-era attacks on Americans racialized as "Asian" were perpetrated by ARBs, for example; and in the autumn of 2022 Los Angeles was rocked by racist remarks directed at a child racialized as "Black" by members of the Los Angeles City Council racialized as "Latino." The social media feeds of Frank James, who massacred over one dozen people in the New York City subway system in 2022, were filled with hateful rants against not only other Americans racialized as "Black" but also against Americans racialized as "White," especially those of Jewish background, Americans racialized as "Latino" and others. Racism is a sort of psychological malfunction, a bug in the machine, which can infect anyone, anywhere. As regards sexism, it should not shock the reader for me to say that many women harbor injurious prejudices about men, as do the young about the old (or the old about the young).

Yet if racism (and sexism, ageism, and etc.) is flowing in all directions in American society, back and forth among all definable groups, it is a greater problem for those who fall into groups which are a *minority* of the population than for those in the *majority* population. As a simple matter of arithmetic, those in minority groups, however defined, will face more people with potentially negative attitudes toward them than those in the majority group. Additionally, the majority group will have more sway in setting the rules of society. Minority groups, if their differing perspectives correlate to different preferences about the organization of society, will have to adjust to outcomes, even if democratically determined (in the sense of "majority rules") that may not suit their wishes. Further, prejudicial feelings held by those who have traditionally held more power and authority, and continue to do so (males of European ancestry) are far more likely to inflict harm than prejudicial feelings held by those who are, in the aggregate, relatively powerless.

For these reasons and others, an ongoing and continuous effort to overcome racist and sexist mindsets is paramount. Such backward ideas must be confronted, examined and continually purged. I strongly believe that a more enlightened humanity is possible. It simply requires a concerted and sustained effort, good will and a sure knowledge of our destination. We Americans have witnessed great strides over the last couple of centuries: with the end of slavery and apartheid, child labor and murderous sweatshops; with equal rights for women; with greater respect for minoritarian sexual and gender identities; with a new-found commitment to the protection of all life on earth; and on many other fronts. In regard to countering racial, ethnic and gender prejudice, the question for a social democrat like myself is how to engage in this ongoing and vital work in such a way that it does not interfere with, if not completely torpedo, the sense of common purpose vital to the project of social democracy.

I will propose, in coming chapters, a social democratic vision for America that, by scrupulously ensuring that all *individuals* enjoy an equal opportunity to fully participate in the economic, social, political and cultural life of their communities and nation, and by fostering a spirit of inclusion and solidarity, will diminish if not completely eliminate the impulse toward tribal competition in the United States. Later we will touch on how this social democratic vision intersects with the particular struggles faced by women, as our culture moves away from its age-old patriarchal model and gendered divisions of labor, and with historically disfavored groups as defined by race-ethnicity. Fostering equal treatment for all is central to social democracy. But if we break society into competing groups, we lose the sense of social solidarity which is absolutely crucial to its implementation and success. Figuring out how to thread that needle will be part of the work of the coming pages.

Most Social Democrats Are "Progressives," But Not All "Progressives" Are Social Democrats . . .

The term "progressive" has become deeply embedded in our political discourse. It even carries the weight of officialdom, with the U.S. House of Representative's "Progressive Caucus" boasting some 95 members as of this writing. I find this unfortunate, since the term is impossibly vague. From a purely semantic point of view, who does not claim to be in favor or "progress?" Donald Trump claims to be for "progress": only for him "progress" means reducing taxes on the wealthy, gutting social protections, despoiling the natural world, applauding dictators, supporting police brutality and keeping out immigrants.

From a policy standpoint, it is hard to find a core program of social organization among self-defined progressives. A number of the better-known members of the House Progressive Caucus are both self-professed "socialists" and members of the Democratic Socialists of America (Alexandria Ocasio-Cortez, Rashida Tlaib, Jamaal Bowman). These political actors, then, would appear to be professing *socialism*. Others appear to follow a more *social democratic* line, yet they do not refer to themselves as social democrats. When we place both "socialists" and "social democrats" under the same rubric, we hopelessly blur the essential distinction between two diametrically opposed ideologies (that is, whether we believe in a state-owned and controlled or a "private enterprise" economic model). Among non-politician, self-proclaimed "progressives," culture-war elements appear to play a large part: defense of LGBTQ+ rights; support for abortion rights; gun control; and redress for racial and gender discrimination. All of these causes are worthy, but these ad hoc policy positions do not constitute a comprehensive program for the economic and political organization of society. A social democrat may share many of the convictions of those who refer to themselves as "progressives." But self-proclaimed "progressives" may not necessary subscribe to the core tenets of social democracy. It is to those core tenets that we now turn.

Defining Social Democracy:

What Social Democracy IS

Social Democracy IS "Social Insurance," or the "Safety Net"

The trait most widely identified with social democracy is something political scientists have traditionally referred to as "social insurance." The underlying idea behind "social insurance" is that each of us, as we make our way through life, are likely to encounter setbacks for which we cannot provide in advance. The most salient of these include illness; loss of a job (and, with it, our means of livelihood); poverty; and old age. In the late 19th Century some European governments, and most famously Germany under Chancellor Otto von Bismarck, decided that government should provide "insurance" to its citizens against such hazards of life. In regard to the four salient life hazards just mentioned, this "insurance" would take the form of government-sponsored healthcare, unemployment insurance, income support programs ("welfare") and old-age pensions. With social insurance programs it might be said that a nation's citizens, through their tax contributions to government, mutually insure one another against unexpected hazards for which most individuals do not have the means to provide on their own. In the United States we are more apt to discuss these aspects of social democracy under the rubric of the "social safety net."

After the turn of the 20th Century, social insurance programs became commonplace in most technologically advanced nations, with varying degrees of coverage. It was in those European nations most associated with social democracy that these programs eventually reached their fullest expression, with universal healthcare coverage, fulsome unemployment benefits, and old-age pensions.

Social Democracy IS Democracy, Solidarity and Inclusion

In his wonderful volume, *Social Democratic America*, Lane Kenworthy writes that "social democracy means a commitment to extensive use of government policy to promote economic security, expand opportunity, and rising living standards for all. But it aims to do so while facilitating freedom, flexibility, and market dynamism." Speaking about the Scandinavian countries famous for social democracy, he writes the following: "There are regulations to protect workers, consumers, and the environment, to be sure. But these exist within an institutional context that aims to encourage entrepreneurship and flexibility by making it easy to start or close a business, to hire or fire employees, and to adjust work hours." In *The Primacy of Politics: Social Democracy and the Making of Europe's Twentieth Century*, Sheri Berman, one of the foremost scholars of social democracy, writes, "European countries emerging from the tragedy of the inter-war years and the Second World War confronted the challenge of creating a world in which the market's reach and excesses could be controlled and people's longing for social solidarity could be satisfied—without the sacrifice of democracy and the trampling of freedom that fascism and Nazism [and also communism, I would add] brought in their wake."

As these excerpts from both Kenworthy and Berman indicate, social democracy is sometimes conflated with the modern welfare state, and not without justification. Nations which are considered to be social democracies by political scientists uniformly provide a robust social safety net against such hazards of human existence as sickness, injury, unemployment and old age. But in order to fully understand the core of social democracy, it is necessary to explore the ideals that inform it.

One of these ideals, to state what may be obvious, is *democracy*. Social democrats believe in representative democracy, participatory politics and the rule of law. We reject the path taken by such socialist heroes as Vladmir Lenin and Fidel Castro, who claimed to be doing good things for their nations by establishing dictatorships and ruthlessly suppressing all dissenting opinions. We will look more closely at the "democracy" piece of social democracy in a coming chapter.

Two further concepts vital to social democracy, less obvious perhaps, are *solidarity* and *inclusion*. These concepts are, in fact, the core drivers behind the social democratic ideal. Solidarity expresses the idea that we, the citizens of a nation, are "in this together." It does not mean that there can be no differences in wealth, or "from each according to his abilities and to each according to his needs," as the communists used to say. But it expresses the idea that we are each of us, to some degree, interdependent with one another, and that none of us can be utterly unconcerned about the fate of *any* of us.

Consider this: in our modern world, with its minute division of labor, before we have been awake for even ten minutes we have relied upon thousands if not millions of other Americans.[1] Flipping a switch to turn on the light, we are benefiting from the labor of everyone working for the power utility, as well as the electricians who originally installed the wiring not only in our home but throughout our neighborhood. We are in the debt of the thousands who were involved in the manufacture of the light bulb, from those who extracted the raw materials from the earth to the factory and administrative workers at the light bulb company; of the drivers who transported the bulb to local warehouses and retail establishments; and of the many retail workers who made the bulb available for purchase. We have already involved ourselves with these many fellow citizens, and we have only gotten so far as turning on the light! Proceeding to the bathroom to shower and shave, we now must rely upon the legions who make possible the myriad plumbing fixtures involved, the water supply, the

1. In our modern, globalized world, we also benefit from the labors of millions of people from other nations, but this is a topic for another book.

manufacture of soap, shampoo, razor, shaving cream, and on it goes. Put differently, "no man (or woman) is an island."

So, merely from the point of view of self-interest, it would seem wise to be concerned that none of our fellow citizens, upon whom we rely for our every daily need, fall through the cracks. Further, beyond the strictly economic roles that our fellow citizens play in our lives, we rely upon one another on a more basic level—that is, to simply follow our society's laws and be good citizens. But even without these justifications of self-interest, it is my conviction that we are, most of us, endowed with a natural caring for our fellow human beings. From this it follows that we feel badly when we learn that one of our number—even be it a complete stranger—is suffering. I am not suggesting that we are responsible for every ill undergone by our neighbors, nor that we are responsible for solving each and every problem encountered by one of our fellow citizens. I simply posit, here, that most human beings wish to live in a society that is not merely *efficient*, and is not merely *just*, but is also *humane*.

The ideal of *solidarity* expresses this natural tendency in most human beings to care about one another. It also expresses the idea that for a group of people engaged in a common enterprise (such as state or nation), a spirit of "one for all, and all for one" strikes a resonant chord in most of us, producing energy and enthusiasm.

The ideal of *inclusion* is closely related to that of solidarity, but reflects the active side of our propensity as human beings to wish to function together as a group. Many of us are especially concerned these days about those who have been marginalized or excluded from participation in various areas of life: be it education, politics, business or the arts. We might say that *solidarity* expresses an underlying feeling of inter-relatedness that informs our actions, while *inclusion* represents the *actions* we take based on that sense of solidarity with our fellow human beings. And in my ideal of social democracy, we will practice not merely inclusion, but what I like to call *radical* inclusion. This principle can be stated as follows:

> Our institutions and laws must be so constructed and applied so that every citizen, to the extent possible, has an *absolutely* equal opportunity to participate in the (1) social, (2) cultural, (3) economic and (4) political life of the community, state and nation. As will be developed in the pages to come, this means that our government institutions must proactively establish programs to ensure that all children have equal developmental and educational opportunities; that young adults have equal access to both education, career training and jobs; and that all who are willing to participate in the economy are compensated at a level allowing them to fully participate in our culture and society.

Social Democracy IS the Public Function, the "Commons" and Worker Representation

From the fact that social democrats believe ardently in democracy we can extrapolate certain other major tenets. During the French presidential elections of 2017 several candidates on the right were promising, as a part of their platforms, budget savings through the reduction of government posts. This became one of the themes of the campaign, and journalists began to ask each of the candidates about their plans in this regard. I was impressed one evening, while watching news from France on the national network France 2, how Benoit Hamon, the candidate of the French Socialist Party (which is today a social democracy party, despite its vestigial name) responded to a reporter's question about how many government posts he wished to suppress. "But I *believe* in the public function," Hamon replied, refusing to go along with the game.

Because social democrats believe in representative democracy, believing it to be the best possible way to give everyone some say in how society is organized, we also believe in the governments elected by this process. We believe, along with the drafters of the U.S. Constitution, that the government represents the "people" in the collective sense and that it operates on our behalf. We do not share, with the American Right, an adversarial role toward government. Instead we believe that government is absolutely necessary to prevent life from devolving into chaos and violence, and also that the government can, ideally, actualize our fondest wishes for a society which is efficient, just and humane. We, like Hamon, "believe in the government function." Feeling that the government is the legitimate carrier of the wishes of the "people," we are not uncomfortable with the expression of that democratically expressed will through government programs and action. For a social democrat the government, acting for "the people," need not apologize for regulating business activity or for taxing wealth and income at whatever level the "people" deem appropriate. That is not to say that a government can never overreach or over-spend, or that we should not be vigilant about those individual rights which are part and parcel of America's political heritage. It merely means that we do not harbor the preconceived notion that government action is likely to be wrongheaded, excessive or unjustified.

Another important concept associated with social democracy is the idea of "the Commons." This term represents everything in the life of our communities and nation which does not rightly belong to private individuals but to us all. Examples of already recognized "Commons" are the air we breath, the water in our rivers, oceans and aquifers, and public parks and wilderness areas. I will develop, in a later chapter, a more expansive, social democratic view of the Commons, which will include these as well as other common resources. We will see how this idea of the Commons can help protect the natural environment and curb global warming.

Finally, since social democracy is based on a private-enterprise model of economic activity, there will always be a potential imbalance of power in the workplace. Under the rawest form of this model, those entrepreneurs (valuable fellow citizens who take the initiative to make things happen) who start and operate businesses are in charge, while those whom they employ to work in their enterprises are at their mercy for wages and work conditions. A major plank in the solution to this imbalance—labor unions— was recognized in the 19th Century and fully codified in the United States under FDR with the National Labor Relations Act. That historic legislation not only established legal protections for workers seeking to organize; it also established the principle that management must be willing to work with labor's elected representatives. Social democrats are committed to the idea that workers must have some say in what goes on in their workplaces and their work lives, and we feel that the proper mechanism with which to ensure this input is labor unions. I will develop this idea further in a later chapter, where we will look at how one advanced social democracy, Germany, makes labor unions a key element in their collective dialogue.

Social Democracy IS Just and Humane: On Human Nature

It would seem axiomatic that any system we propose to regulate society must, if it is to be successful, comport with human nature. It would seem equally true that the more completely a system of social organization comports with human nature, the more durable that system will be and the more content will be the people who live within it. Human nature, of course, is variable, but for almost every trait (aggressiveness, risk aversion, altruism) a bell curve will reveal a large mass of individuals clustered in the middle of the spectrum, indicating a medium range within which most people fall for that trait. Under a Bentham-like analysis, a social system based upon the nature of this normative mass of individuals will best produce the "greatest good for the greatest number."

Some animal species, such as bees, are almost completely communal in nature. Only one bee in a hive, the queen, reproduces, and each of the thousands of other bees in the hive work tirelessly to keep the queen safe and to care for the young she bears. Each bee will die to protect the hive without the slightest hesitation. On the other end of the spectrum we have animals like the mountain lion: a true loner. Unlike African lions, for example, the American cougar does not live in prides. In fact, cougars have as little to do with one another as possible. Each animal patrols and guards an individual territory from which it violently excludes others. The only time two cougars get together is during rare periods of female estrus, when biological necessity requires a brief fling after which the male sulks off, never again to see, or be concerned with, either the female he has just mated with or the offspring she will bear. The mother will of course travel with her young when they are immature and still learning to hunt. But once the offspring are self-sufficient, they go on their way to take up the same lonely existence followed by their parents.

It would seem too obvious to require stating that we human beings are neither as communal in nature as bees nor as solitary in nature as mountain lions. We have our own selfish interests, but we also demonstrate a marked tendency to care about others and to be willing to work for the good of our communities. The red-letter day in the life of Robinson Crusoe, shipwrecked on a desert island, was the day he encountered Friday, another human being. We are constitutionally (genetically, if you will) ill-equipped to live away from our co-specifics. Nor can we help but care about them. The photograph of a child suffering from starvation, a child we will never meet who lives thousands of miles away, will move us deeply. The most cursory review of history and cultures from around the world will tell us that humans invariably organize themselves into groups, with lines of authority and common purposes.

The writer Arthur Koestler used the term *holon* to describe an entity that is both a whole in itself and part of a larger whole, and I believe that this well describes human beings.

We each feel ourselves to be individuals, with our own idiosyncratic ideas, thoughts, feelings, wants and desires. But we also feel ourselves to be part of such larger units as couples, families, communities, nations and even, for many of us, the whole of humanity.

A social system which will both endure and bring the greatest good to the greatest number must comport with this dual nature of human beings: that is, as both individualistic and communal beings. Social democrats believe that true socialists err in treating human beings as if we were a purely communal species, like bees, while free-marketeers err in treating human beings as if we were a completely individualistic species, like mountain lions. The project of social democracy is to build societies which answer to both the communal and the individualistic sides of our nature.

The English philosopher John Locke (1632-1704) had an outsized influence on the founders of the United States, and his ideas continue to mold the thinking of many conservatives. Locke was not sanguine about human beings' capacity for goodness. He believed that we are essentially self-centered. As such, the best that government can do, in Locke's view, is to keep these self-centered individuals from too greatly damaging one another. Government can do this, according to Locke, by enforcing laws against such obvious harm as batteries, murder and theft, and also by enforcing contracts (making people keep their word) or prosecuting fraud (penalizing lying). To expect people to actually care about others as much as they care about themselves, for a Lockean conservative, is unrealistic, and any system of social organization based on this fond hope will, according to those who bear the Lockean philosophy, fail.

We social democrats disagree with Lockean conservatives. We grant them that human beings are not a completely communal species, and that to expect them to care only about others (or a communist "collective") is folly. We utterly reject the notion, however, that we are not capable of caring about the fate of others. Untold acts of selflessness, witnessed all around us every day, bely such a notion. Further proof is the support, in the United States, for programs based on communal feeling (social security, scholarships for poor children, aid for the disabled), as well as the documented contentment of people living in the advanced social democracies of Scandinavia, nations which consistently top lists of citizen happiness.[2]

Decades of involvement with my fellow citizens tells me that the average American feels at least some level of both sadness and distress when we learn of, or witness, the suffering of a fellow citizen. If we conclude, it is true, that the individual concerned brought upon their suffering through improvident, unwise or immoral behavior, we may decide that there is nothing we can do to help, because to do so would only enable more improvident, unwise or immoral behavior. But if, on the other hand, we conclude that the individual suffers through no fault of their own, our compassion is undiluted and our desire to help greater (this is the dichotomy, common in welfare discourse, of the "deserving" vs. the "undeserving" poor). In any case, I argue that Americans (the vast majority of us, anyway, in the middle of the bell curve) are at least somewhat compassionate by nature. For this reason, we will feel uncomfortable living in a society where suffering, particularly the suffering of blameless individuals, is not addressed. Considered in this light, support for a humane society does in fact have a selfish component: for it spares each of us the uncomfortable feelings attendant upon watching others suffer unjustly.

---

2. See Pew Research: Views of the Economic System and the Social Safety Net (https://www.pewresearch.org/politics/2019/12/17/views-of-the-economic-system-and-social-safety-net/) ; YouGov: How Americans evaluate Social Security, Medicare, and six other entitlement programs (https://today.yougov.com/topics/politics/articles-reports/2023/02/08/americans-evaluate-social-security-medicare-poll); Most oppose Social Security, Medicare cuts: AP-NORC poll (https://apnews.com/article/social-security-medicare-cuts-ap-poll-biden-9e7395e8efeab68063d741beac6ef24b).

Another apparently innate characteristic of human beings pertinent to our social democratic project is a desire for justice.[3] It is likely that hundreds of thousands of years of evolving in small groups, where we were intimately dependent upon one another, where resources were scarce and where the fair distribution of the group's productive effort was a matter of life or death, have left us with a strong commitment to fairness—and an equally intense distaste for injustice. Not only do we feel indignant when we ourselves are treated unfairly, but the vast majority of us feel distinctly uncomfortable when we see others treated unfairly. For this reason, most human beings prefer to live in societies which are fair and just.

Social democracy, then, can be seen as a system of social organization which recognizes our dual nature as both an individualistic and a communal species, and which honors our desire to live in a society which is both just and humane.

Defining Social Democracy: Is the United States a Social Democracy?

Having now, the author hopes, brought some clarity to the questions of both what social democracy is not and what it is, let's take a moment to consider whether the United States might be considered a social democratic nation. The United States is not generally mentioned when political scientists, economists and journalists discuss social democracy, but if we survey the organization of American society, as well as government programs that impact the welfare of its citizens, we will find many elements that fit within social democracy's general definition. First, we are a democracy, if an imperfect one. Secondly, there is a private-enterprise economic system. Finally, the United States possesses several of the social safety net programs common to social democracy: these include old-age pensions (Social Security); unemployment insurance; assistance for those in poverty (Temporary Assistance for

---

3. Jon Wisman, *The Origins and Dynamics of Inequality*, pp. 9-10 & 61-64.

Needy Families, Supplemental Nutrition Assistance Program, Medicaid); aid for the disabled (Social Security disability assistance); and others. In 2010 the United States took a significant step toward another hallmark program of social democracies: universal health care.[4]

The question naturally arises why, possessing so many hallmarks of social democracy, the United States is not generally considered to be among the club of social democratic nations. I will stipulate, first, that it is possible for a nation to be social democratic by degrees: slightly social democratic, moderately social democratic, or largely social democratic. Within this spectrum, I would argue that the United States is moderately social democratic. Another way to view the issue is through the maturity of a system. In this context, I would classify the United States as an incipient rather than mature social democracy, with about half of its political actors (Democrats) straining towards a fuller social democracy and the

4 Socialist parties were weak in early 20th Century America, as compared to Europe, and it was not until the Great Depression that laissez-faire doctrines were seriously challenged here. Under the strain of that crisis, FDR (claiming, famously, that he was acting to save capitalism) spearheaded the erection of the initial pillars of social democracy in the United States: the National Labor Relations Act (guaranteeing collective bargaining rights); Social Security; national unemployment insurance; a national minimum wage; and Aid for Families with Dependant Children (welfare). Also important, though temporary, were active labor market programs like the Works Progress Administration and the Civilian Conservation Corps, which put the unemployed back to work. Though public health insurance was a chief priority for FDR's successor, Harry Truman, he failed to convince a Republican Congress; it was not until the presidency of Lyndon Baynes Johnson that social democracy received another major boost in the form of Medicare and Medicaid. Throughout the remainder of the 1960s and into the 70s, American social democracy benefited from such enhancements to the social safety net as food stamps and expanded housing vouchers, as well as one major new pillar—the Earned Income Tax Credit, which lifts many working families out of poverty. The next major breakthrough occurred with President Obama's Affordable Care Act.

other half (Republicans) fighting against further steps toward a more completely social democratic America.

Though the United States' social safety net contains many, if not most, of the elements found in mature social democracies, we will find that these programs are typically less comprehensive, and provide less security for our citizens, than those of the more mature social democracies of Europe. If we take unemployment insurance as an example, U.S. benefits are extremely stingy. The average benefit for all states is just $370 per week, or about $1,600 per month. This is not enough to support a single person in major metropolitan areas, to say nothing of parents with dependent children. Benefits typically run out at six months, regardless of whether work has been found. By comparison, many unemployment programs in European nations provide benefits for up to two years, with payments replacing a greater share of lost income.[5]

Looking at healthcare, mature social democracies ensure that every citizen is covered, either through a single-payer national health service (as in Britain) or through subsidized private insurance. The Affordable Care Act was a major step toward the ideal of universal healthcare for Americans, but tens of millions of our nation's citizens still lack coverage, and premiums for private insurance offered through the program's exchanges are forbidding for many. Those with too little income to qualify for ACA plans may in some cases receive healthcare through Medicaid, but in those states which did not take the Medicaid Expansion under the Act, many at the lowest end of the income spectrum have no access other than hospital emergency rooms on a charitable basis. Considering other areas, the Scandinavian nations provide highly subsidized childcare for working parents; and 12 weeks of paid family leave is commonplace throughout western Europe. Education, through college level, is largely free for citizens of the most mature social democracies, and in some countries

5. See https://data.oecd.org/benwage/benefits-in-unemployment-share-of-previous-income.htm; https://www.economist.com/special-report/2021/04/08/the-case-for-danish-welfare.

students even receive government stipends for living expenses.

So, merely by comparing the level of "social insurance" provided by the United States as compared to that provided by the mature social democracies of Europe, as well as the support for such basic needs as childcare for working parents and education, we see that the United States has only traveled part of the road toward social democracy. But I believe there are also other, more subtle indicators which explain why the United States is not typically described as a social democracy. One of these is our nation's political discourse, both among political actors and among the general population. Neither French president Emmanuel Macron nor recently retired German Chancellor Angela Merkel, though both are considered center-right by European standards (both would be Hillary Clinton Democrats in the United States) would ever consider proposing that their nations' universal healthcare guarantees be dismantled, that their old-age pension systems be privatized, or that laws be passed which make it difficult for workers to organize in unions. That is to say, the social democratic programs developed in these and other European nations since the Second World War are considered indelible features of the social contract; they are not questioned. Surely there is debate about how to best and most efficiently run social insurance programs and other government services, but the rightness of the basic social democratic model is not up for negotiation. The contrast with the United States need hardly be pointed out, where about half of our political actors (Republicans) subscribe to a libertarian, free-market ideology in which the state takes little or no responsibility for such human needs as healthcare, support during periods of unemployment, family leave or higher education, and where a key goal is to destroy the capacity of workers to find a voice at the workplace through union representation.

Related to America's fractured political discourse around social democracy, informing it while also being informed by it, is the lack of a shared commitment to the ideals, discussed above, of solidarity and inclusion. "Solidarity," a word seldom heard in American political discourse, is a constantly used benchmark in European social democracies (France possesses a Ministry of Solidarity and Health; Spain's tax on large fortunes is called the "Solidarity Tax"). Laws and government programs are evaluated, in countries such as Spain and France, based upon the perceived effects such laws and programs might have on "solidarity." Solidarity, the feeling among a community or nation's citizens that they, at least to some substantial extent, are "in this together," that the welfare of each, to some substantial extent, depends upon the welfare of all, is considered, and spoken of, as a tangible substance. For Europe's mature social democracies, solidarity is a priceless good that must be fostered, nurtured and preserved. Factors that damage solidarity (for example, leaving workers in the lurch when a factory closes and moves overseas) are to be avoided, while those elements that enhance solidarity (creating a plan to support the workers of the abandoned factory) are promoted. With solidarity comes heartfelt commitment to community and nation. When solidarity is absent or damaged, citizens see themselves as lone agents with no sense of responsibility for a wider community: one which has shown no concern for them. And for true solidarity, a social democratic nation must tend to the closely related principle of inclusion. We cannot have true solidarity when some are left out. The mature social democracy will not merely pay lip service to inclusion. It will act, continually, intentfully and proactively, to ensure that all citizens have an equal opportunity to participate in the social, cultural, economic and political life of their community and nation.

Beginning in the early 20th Century, and particularly with FDR's New Deal, the United States began to add social democratic elements to our system of socio-political organization. But it has been a hard-fought struggle against rightist political actors and their adherents, a struggle which is as intense at this writing as ever. Not only must each incremental gain be fought hard for, but with the nation evenly divided between right and left, each achieved gain is always in danger of being reversed. Social democracy will only reach maturity in America, and be secure in its victory, when a critical mass of the voting public (significantly greater than the +/-50% which Democrats can now count on at the polls) have internalized the values of solidarity and inclusion, and when they understand, believe in and support the social democratic model as the system most likely to give those values substance.

Part II

Nuts & Bolts

Nuts and Bolts

Having considered what social democracy means in a general sense, I will devote the remainder of this volume to some concrete proposals for increasing social democracy in America. We will begin with the centrality of work.

The Centrality of Work

In commencing this discussion of concrete proposals for implementing a fuller social democratic system in the United States with the centrality of work, I do not mean to imply that work is more important than such other aspects of our lives as family, friends, leisure or, for example, the study of philosophy. But inasmuch as social democracy is a system of *political* and *economic* organization, not a scheme for the organization of one's entire life, we limit our focus here to those areas where our lives interact with the political and economic system in which we live. And for most of us, by far and away the most important manner in which we interact with society is through our work lives. Not only do we achieve material security and comfort through our jobs, for most people work also provides a vital sense of belonging and purpose.

Work in our social democratic American future will represent the social democratic values we have established: it will respond to and enhance feelings of *solidarity* and *inclusion*; it will be both *just* and *humane*; and it will allow ordinary citizens a say in the conditions under which they work.

The Current American System of Work Falls Short of Social Democratic Ideals

The system of working life under which American citizens currently live falls short of our social democratic values on several fronts. In almost any period of history there are not enough jobs to go around, so that some must suffer unemployment and loss of income, which offends the values of justice, solidarity and inclusion. Many of the jobs that do exist are compensated at wages that do not afford a life considered dignified by the average person; this not only offends the values of justice, solidarity and inclusion, but also demonstrates a lack of humane concern for our fellow citizens. Many American states have made it difficult for unions to operate, which violates the social democratic ideal that average workers should have a say in the conditions of their work lives. And due to circumstances of birth, some individuals have access to career opportunities not available to others: this violates the principles of both justice and solidarity.

Low Wages and Marx's "Reserve Army of the Unemployed"

Before we proceed to how to amend this state of affairs, let's look closely at the two most problematic areas of American worklife from a social democratic perspective: unemployment and inadequate wages. As we will see, the two are related.

I believe that Marx was divorced from the realities of human nature when he suggested that human beings could function successfully under communism. He did, however, provide us with some useful concepts and analytic tools. Among the best of these, to my mind, is the idea of the "reserve army of the unemployed." Marx understood that as long as there is a large pool of unemployed workers, desperate to make any income at all, already-employed workers at the low end of the skills scale will have little or no bargaining power over their wages and work conditions. The employer will have scant incentive to respond to demands for higher pay or better work conditions if the worker can easily be replaced by others desperate enough to accept any wage offered and under any terms. (Inversely, if labor is in short supply, employees have considerable bargaining power: the employer, threatened with the loss of an employee, with little prospect for replacing them, will have a great incentive to cede to demands for higher wages or better working conditions. During the recent pandemic we have seen exactly this mechanism in operation, as large American companies like McDonald's, in the face of pandemic-related labor shortage, raised wages significantly to attract workers.)

At any given time there are typically several million individuals looking for work but unable to find jobs. This number can, during economic downturns such as the 2008 recession, balloon to ten percent or more of the entire labor force. This represents tens of millions of our fellow citizens who have lost the income they rely upon to pay rents and mortgages, feed their children and attend to the other necessities of living. Unemployment insurance seldom comes even close to replacing the lost income.[1]

When we operate under a system in which the only way to obtain the necessities of life is through a job, and where there are typically fewer jobs than individuals who need them—a number which at times can rise into the tens of millions—we are participating in a cruel game of musical chairs: cruel because this is not a game, but people's lives, families, health and futures which are at stake.

Those on the conservative side of the political spectrum are not overly troubled by this state of affairs. They will tell you, first of all, that those who are unemployed could find a job if they really tried. This, I concede, is sometimes true: there are those who game the unemployment system. But there are many more who don't. Especially during economic downturns, or when a factory which employs half of a small town's workers relocates overseas, the jobs simply *are not there.* Not even the most committed conservative, I imagine, would have the nerve to say that during the massive recession of 2008-2009, when the number of unemployed shot up from five to ten percent, that the millions of additional unemployment claimants were merely *faking* it; or that during the Great Depression, when nearly one third of the American workforce was out of work, that these struggling citizens, who had

1. See p. 30, above.

worked their entire lives, had suddenly decided to *pretend* they couldn't find a job.

Most conservatives will, then, likely concede that there are times when there simply are not enough jobs to go around (in reality, this is "most of the time"). But in the "law of the jungle" mental universe in which today's rightists operate, this problem comes under the heading of "tough luck." The laissez-faire, unrestrained free-market philosophy of most Republican politicians today posits that when there are fewer jobs than workers, the strong will survive and the weak will be thrown under the bus where, if they are not crushed, they will somehow straggle along in a further weakened state.

In any case (the Right will further argue) even if persistent unemployment is cruel and unfair, anything that we might do to prevent or solve the problem will only make matters worse. If we offer generous unemployment insurance, workers will have no incentive to seek jobs, thereby creating labor shortages, bottlenecks in the economy, inflation and diminished output. And if the government were to get involved in guaranteeing employment, this would lead to "socialism" and an intrusion of the inefficient public sector into the "efficient" private sector, thus dooming us all to a lower standard of living. Put differently, we would be interfering with the unhindered operation of the marketplace, which for the hardcore conservative is the best and fairest possible regulator of society.

It probably need not be stated that I, a social democrat, reject these conservative arguments. First, I believe that we can protect citizens from the hazards associated with unemployment without diminishing output and prosperity (I am convinced, in fact, and will develop further below, that we will *increase* prosperity if the average worker is better taken care of).[2] But more fundamentally, even if an unfettered laissez-faire system could deliver marginally more production—which I deny—flowing in out-sized proportions to a wealthy minority,

2. In this context, see the *Economist* article cited p. 30 on Denmark, whose unemployment payments are among the most generous in the world and its labor market among the world's strongest.

this could serve as no justification for a cruel and inhumane system. We can make calculations about many things and do cost-benefit analyses, but a cost-benefit analysis is not generally the proper model for making moral choices. We do not decide whether to murder someone, or cheat on our spouse, with cost-benefit analyses (at least most of us would agree that we shouldn't). We make a moral decision, and we would not murder someone no matter how low the cost ("you'll never get caught") or high the reward ("you'll inherit the one hundred million"). To leave some segment of our fellow citizens in the lurch, with no means to support themselves and their families, is *morally* wrong. Such a system should, therefore, not even be on the table, no more than should be murdering your brother to get the inheritance, even if you knew you could get away with it.

The question then remains as to how we solve the related problems of low wages and unemployment. But before getting to concrete proposals, allow me one further digression: into the children's story of the *Little Red Hen*. I bring this story in now, because it forms a backdrop to many of my ideas about work in a functioning social democracy.

The Little Red Hen

The story of the Little Red Hen, a Russian folk tale which I read, or had read to me as a toddler in the late 1950s, is quite simple. In one version, the Little Red Hen decides to make a cake, and she invites all of the other barnyard animals to participate. Each of the critters steps up to take on an assignment, whether it be sowing the wheat, harvesting it, threshing or milling it into flour, mixing the batter or making the icing. But there is one rebel, the grasshopper, who declines to get involved. He would rather, he says, enjoy himself leaping around in the sun-splashed fields than take on any tedious labor. The Little Red Hen makes no objection at the time, but when the tasty cake is finally completed and the grasshopper reappears, asking for a slice, the Little Red Hen announces her timeless dictum: those who do not help *make* the cake shall not help *eat* the cake.

Even as a child I perceived the essential *rightness* of the Little Red Hen's position. None of us appreciate the housemate who shirks chores, or the friend who always seems to be broke when the check comes at the restaurant. That is, we expect everyone to be willing to work toward a shared outcome if they expect to participate in the benefits on offer. This answers to what I believe is an innate sense of fairness, developed over eons of living together in social groups, in *homo sapiens*. From a social democratic point of view, the idea that those who wish to share in the products of labor should be willing to contribute to its creation answers to the ideal of *justice*.

This view places me squarely at odds with those on the left who advocate for universal incomes, or those who complain about work mandates under Temporary Assistance for Needy Families (TANF), the federal program which replaced Aid for Families with Dependent Children (AFDC) during the Clinton administration. Even Marxists believe that the fruits of labor should be enjoyed by those who contribute that labor: this is why they excoriate capitalists who, in their view, co-opt the fruits of labor provided by workers. And it is not only the social democratic ideal of *justice* that is threatened when some live off the labor of others. It will be remembered that the social democratic ideal of *radical inclusion* requires that all citizens have the opportunity to be involved, to the extent possible, in the social, cultural, political and *economic* life of our communities and nation. And it is by working at a job (self-employed or otherwise) that citizens participate in our economy. Working-age adults who do not work suffer marginalization on many levels, as well as loss of social standing and self-esteem. Welfare recipients who were required to take jobs with the changeover from AFDC to TANF in the late 90s reported increased psychological well-being, greater self-esteem and a new sense of pride, particularly in their relations with their children.[3] Another social democratic ideal, *solidarity*, is

3. See Robert Cherry's masterful volume, *Welfare Transformed*, Oxford

also compromised when some are given free money while others must work for it. Those working will resent those who are receiving benefits for nothing, and these resentful voters will not support the social safety net which is vital to social democracy. Studies show that a solid majority of the American public *will* support benefit programs targeted to those they deem to be truly in need of support: the elderly and the handicapped, for example.[4] But most would agree that if *they* need to work to make money, able-bodied others should, too.

A System for Willing Workers in a Social Democratic Future

I began this chapter with the assertion that the American system of work suffers from two primary problems in regard to our social democratic ideals: (1) in any typical period, our economy does not generate a number of jobs equal to those seeking work, depriving millions of our fellow citizens of the means of survival, and (2) the resulting "reserve army of the unemployed" deprives workers at the low end of the skills scale of any power to bargain for higher wages or better working conditions. I have further posited that this situation being a *moral* wrong, we have no choice, if we wish to inhabit a *just* society, but to correct it.

The solution I proffer to these inter-related problems includes, first, a living wage. The second element of the solution is a form of employment guarantee: but unlike many other such proposals, it does not rely on government to supply jobs to make up shortfalls in the private labor market.

Living Wage

First, all jobs in our social democratic future will be required to pay a "living wage." The idea of the living wage is guided by our social democratic ideal of *justice*. It is not *just* to expect people to work all week, providing services necessary to the

University Press, 2007.
4. https://www.axios.com/2023/05/18/axios-ipsos-poll-work-requirements-medicaid-snap

functioning of our economy, and not have enough money at the end of the month to decently maintain themselves. A living wage is also required to satisfy the social democratic ideals of *solidarity* and *inclusion*. Poverty not only brings material hardships of various kinds, it also results in *social marginalization*. Those in poverty often feel shame and exclusion, since the conditions under which they live are considered unacceptable by the majority of their fellow citizens. Their lack of resources precludes participation in cultural and social activities which foster connection to community. Children living in impoverished homes may not feel comfortable inviting friends over; they do not have access to the same clothing, games, electronics and other developmental and social-bond-forming experiences as their better-off peers. These factors result in *exclusion* rather than *inclusion* and diminish feelings of *solidarity* both for the impoverished family and those who look upon them as "other." They lead to depression and other psychological ailments in adults, and for children they leave lasting scars of low self-esteem, impede the development of their potentials and reduce their capacity to contribute as adults.

But how would a "living wage" be calculated, you ask? Without going into great detail here,[5] the living wage, importantly, will be calculated for each zip code, based on cost factors for that locality. Housing typically constitutes a family or individual's greatest monthly expense, and housing costs vary wildly among zip codes: it requires a considerably higher income to stay afloat in the San Francisco Bay area than in rural Mississippi.

Taking into account these local factors (chiefly housing costs), the principle behind the calculation of the living wage would be that no worker should have to live in conditions that the average American would consider unacceptable or

---

5. For one approach to calculating a Living Wage, see the Economic Policy Institute's "Family Budget Calculator," by zip code, here: https://www.epi.org/resources/budget/?gclid=CjwKCAjwh8mlBhB_EiwAsztdBJLkb0NQYr6i9nFsjxPXG2x3DZGTAE1aFRxT6x0mtsJyhh-fx5tnivhoCeLUQAvD_BwE

undignified. More specifically, the living wage would be set so that a single person working a full-time job could rent a one-bedroom apartment which is clean, healthy, with the usual utilities, and maintained to a level of curb appeal that the average American would consider acceptable. (For couples living together, two of these wages would, obviously, command considerably more buying power.) Beyond rent, the living wage would take into account costs of food, healthcare, transportation and other necessities. Consideration would also be given to such social needs as cultural events and leisure, as such experiences foster *solidarity* and *inclusion*. Additional costs associated with children living in the home would be addressed with targeted subsidies for such necessities as school supplies and clothing, as well as cultural and social inclusion.

Such considerations may seem extraordinary to the average American not grappling with poverty wages, as many of us have become inured to the shabby treatment of our fellow citizens. But it must be stressed, lest this seem a form of *welfare*, that we are discussing an appropriate wage for those who are working, not benefits given for nothing: thus the *Little Red Hen* principle is satisfied. If the Little Red Hen decreed that those who did not help make the cake would not help eat the cake, she also made it clear that all those who participated in making the cake *would* share in eating it! Beyond the moral necessity of treating all people decently, material benefits will accrue to all of us when social solidarity and inclusion are increased. Children—the adults of tomorrow—will grow up in homes where their needs are being addressed and potentials developed, thus fostering within them feelings of solidarity and inclusion, leading to a desire to give back to the communities that have nurtured them.

Guaranteed Employment or Training

A living wage will resolve the problem of too low wages for those who are working. But what about the unemployed, who receive no wage? One solution would be to key unemployment benefits to our living wage and make their duration indefinite. This solution, however, would create other problems. First, if unemployment benefits were keyed to a living wage and of indefinite duration, there should be no argument that many people would never look for a job again but would jump at the chance of a life of guaranteed leisure. Many who are working would quit their jobs to acquire such a life, and those already jobless would have little material incentive to seek work. Those who were still working would, like the Little Red Hen, justifiably resent this situation (*solidarity* would be compromised) and would quickly use their votes to end such a program.

So how to maintain the unemployed at a decent level while not incurring the downsides just mentioned? And how best end their marginalization and exclusion, and get them back into participation in the economic life of community and nation? The solution I propose for this is built around federally supported employment agency Hubs, with a guarantee of either (1) a job at a living wage, or (2) training or upskilling, *also paid at a living wage.* First, in each community (this could be a county, a part of a county, a city or ward of a city) there will be located a branch of this joint federal-state employment agency. Second, all employers will be required to post all openings to the agency's national database, so the Employment Hub will be aware of all openings, both within their region and beyond (employers will not be required, however, to hire any given applicant sent from the Hub). The Hub will serve the multiple purposes of employment agency and training coordinator. An individual who is involuntarily unemployed (those who leave a job voluntarily or are dismissed for cause would not be eligible for the system) and unable to find work on their own will come into their local Hub. The job seeker will be enrolled, and if they agree to the program's conditions will immediately begin to receive benefits at a living wage. A Hub counselor will do a thorough evaluation of the job seeker's skill set and education level. Aware of all openings in the area, the counselor will then help the job seeker find openings consistent with their qualifications and help arrange interviews. If, after a set period of time—two months, for example—no employment offers materialize, the counselor will guide the job seeker toward a full-time (minimum 30 in-person[6] hours per week) training or upskilling program consistent with their capacities (and, if possible, interests) and one for which prospects for employment are high. For example, if a region is experiencing a dearth of welders, or of dental technicians, the counselor will steer the applicant in these directions. The client's desires will be considered, but final determination of a particular training program will require sign-off by the counselor. These Employment Hubs will be located at or near community colleges, where they can conveniently integrate their job insertion function into a growing trend of vocational education, closely coordinated with regional employers, already taking place in America's two-year colleges. The job seeker will continue to be available for possible employment during the training program and must take any available job on offer for which they are qualified. Training programs will be organized around short-term modules, however, and in such cases job seekers will be allowed to finish a current module before going back to work.

The job seeker, once in a full-time training (or *upskilling*) program, will be required to attend consistently. If the job seeker fails to attend, or fails to apply themselves, they will be warned, sanctioned and, if they do not improve their participation, washed out of the program.

Counselors will have access to resources for special cases: for example, to help with transportation either to training programs, job interviews or a job itself. (Such measures, by the way, are not unusual in mature social democracies. I watched a story on the French news a few years ago about a young graduate who was seeking work in the area of her major—hotels and hospitality. Unable to find a job in her field, she had <u>recourse to the lo</u>cal branch of France's national employment

6. Online training, done at home, would enable malingering and abuse.

agency, the *Poêle Emploi.* The agency counselor found a suitable position, but it was in another town, some hours away. At this point *Poêle Emploi* intervened to help the job seeker with costs to attend an interview, and she was offered the job. *Poêle Emploi* then helped with relocation costs, including two months rent on an apartment, so that the job seeker could begin her career!)[7]

For many Americans, the system I propose here may seem just too, well, *nice.* And indeed, such a system will support the creation of a society which is *humane,* a key social democratic value. It will also increase *solidarity* and *inclusion,* which benefit all of us: the more people feel committed to their society, and part of it, the more they are likely to follow its laws, pay their taxes properly, engage in volunteer work and otherwise help build strong and happy communities.

In addition to these intangible but priceless benefits, an economic system which is proactively working to insert job seekers into the labor force—and to provide those who need it with training and upskilling—is an economic system that will be running on all cylinders. Economists have been telling us, for several decades, that the pace of technological change we are undergoing requires workers who are lifelong learners. They also tell us that those societies with the most highly trained work forces are the ones that will enjoy the greatest prosperity. This all goes to a critical aspect of our social democratic future: the *development of human capital.* A vibrant, successful society is one which sees its greatest resource in its *people.* Such a society does not stint in making sure all citizens are able to develop and work up to their full potentials, enabling them to most fully contribute to our communities. A successful society will strive to maximize its human capital with measures to ensure its citizens' health and safety, attend to the education of the young and, as here, accompany workers in their quest to perform their most useful function in

---

7. In some cases, for example where local opportunities do not exist, job seekers at the Hubs may need to relocate ourside their region.

our economic life. America could become the human capital champion of the world. The supply of constantly upskilling workers would result in more efficient businesses, greater innovation and happier citizens. And when a foreign manufacturer, for example, is looking to locate a new plant where they can expect a prepared workforce, they would need look no further than the U.S.A.

The Unwilling

I have proposed a system whereby all *willing* workers will be guaranteed either a job at a living wage or, if one cannot be found, a training or upskilling program compensated at that same living wage. But what is to be done, if anything, for those who are unwilling to participate, due either to real obstacles or simple aversion to work? And what about those whose participation is so half-hearted and insincere that the participant is neither contributing on the job nor effectuating any real upskilling? In other words, what is to be done about, first, those who refuse to participate at all and, second, about shirkers and malingerers?

For those who are truly able-bodied and able-minded but refuse to honestly participate (those who try to "game the system") my proposed program has little sympathy. Under the *Little Red Hen* principle, we have no desire to coddle and enable individuals, like the grasshopper, whose goal is to live from the productive efforts of others while making no contribution themselves. Such would-be users, if they are lucky, will find honest workers who, for whatever reason, are willing to share. As citizens, these non-participants will be entitled to basic social insurance benefits common to all, such as healthcare. They will also have access to sex-segregated homeless dormitories, safe and clean but otherwise Spartan, staffed with counselors whose role will be to steer occupants into either constructive effort or, where appropriate, facilities for the psychologically ill and/or substance addicted. All who wish to have cash wages, however, must be willing to make an honest effort at performing a job, if available, or if not at upskilling.[8]

But what of those whose family exigencies or personal difficulties would complicate participation in our guaranteed work-or-training system? Let's first consider single parents with dependent children. This is a group that we might say has a legitimate reason why they would be reluctant to either take a job or participate in a full-time upskilling program. We will solve this problem by providing childcare, both at Employment Hubs and at training and upskilling centers. Once placed in a job, the worker will benefit from a universal system of subsidized childcare, such as that proposed in President Biden's "Build Back Better" plan of 2021. For those with elderly parents to care for, or other disabled, the expansion of our social safety net to include at-home care will be key.

A more difficult question is what to do about those who participate but do so at an inadequate level of dedication. We can easily envision individuals who will gain placement in an upskilling program but fail to attend regularly or carry out assignments. There will also be those who achieve employment through the Employment Hubs but then miss work or fail to perform to an appropriate level on the job. It should be recalled, here, that employers will be under no obligation to either hire applicants sent to them from Employment Hubs or maintain them on their payrolls if they do not perform at the required level. Employment counselors, with input from trainers and employers, will determine whether the participant's inadequate performance is due to unwillingness to make an effort or is due to such more acceptable reasons as a mismatch between skills and job function or some physical, mental or psychological incapacity. If it is determined that the job "seeker" is simply not willing to put out an effort, they will be washed out of the system. As a further backstop to

---

8. A difficult issue will arise when the unwilling are parents. If the refusal of parents to participate in work or training at a living wage leads to harmful levels of deprivation for a child, the result would be referral to child welfare agencies, with foster care the likely solution.

prevent such "free riders" from gaming the system, we could limit both the length and number of times a citizen can employ the Hub, with this threshold adjustable to account for fluctuations in the unemployment level. The compensation of Hub employment counselors will be tied to the number of successful job placements made, so these professionals will be highly incentivized to weed out the unserious and get the truly willing into gainful employment.

As a basic rule, job seekers will be required to take any available job for which they possess the capacity and skills: and remember that all jobs will be paid, at a minimum, at a "living wage" as defined by a system such as that employed by the Economic Policy Institute.[9] We could soften this rule by allowing job seekers to pass on the first two or three offers or, once or twice per lifetime, to stay within the Employment Hub for a period of up to, say, one year in upskilling while attempting to secure a job in their chosen field. During his first term in office, President Macron of France proposed such a system of "social accounts," whereby workers would earn credits for quarters worked (as in Social Security in the U.S.); once a sufficient number of credits are earned, the worker would be entitled to leave work and enroll in a training program for a limited amount of time. This would facilitate mid-life career changes as well as job-skill enhancements. We could employ a similar strategy, basing workers' right to training at a living wage upon credits earned in employment.

In addition to those who are able-bodied and able-minded, there are those who must work with handicaps, whether physical, mental or psychological. Naturally, special accommodations must be made for such individuals. Under the social democratic ideal of *inclusion*, the collective, acting through the state, will want to be proactive in making sure that every individual who wants to participate *can* participate. Employment Hubs and training centers will assess clients' capacities, identify appropriate accommodations, and work with employers to help them benefit from the potentials of citizens

9. See footnote, page 42, above.

whose abilities are different, but not necessary any less valuable, than those of others. As to those unable to function in any work setting, whether due to physical, mental or psychological causes, social insurance programs for the disabled will ensure that they live in a dignified manner.

Before leaving the topic of guaranteed work or training I'd like to address what will no doubt be a standard set of right-wing objections. Firstly, the Right will begin, such a program is not needed because "anyone who really wants a job can find one." This, as I hope I have demonstrated, is not true. During any given time period it is rare that there are enough jobs for everyone who would like to have one. And if we look at specific geographic locations, this statement is often wildly untrue: those places where the employment offer has been gutted by the flight of factories or the cessation of extractive activities like mining, to take two examples. "Even so," our conservative friend will continue, "such a program as you suggest will quickly degenerate into a government bonanza for idlers and shirkers." This objection is more credible, and it is true that we must apply stern measures to prevent people from gaming the system. I believe those I have outlined, if rigorously applied, will suffice. But behind the rightist objection to guaranteed work or training is a more fundamental objection, and it goes to an unspoken belief about the way the labor market should function. A system such as we now use, with a standing "reserve army of the unemployed" prepared to accept low wages and poor work conditions, causing all general-purpose workers (those without specialized, in-demand skills) to live in a sort of desperation bred of precarity,[10] certainly keeps people on their toes. The fear of winding up in this class, or the desire to get out of it, no doubt spurs many to improve their skill base and to be willing to work harder and longer to earn their daily bread. As such, such a system may be one way of maintaining a high-producing economy.

10. The term *precarity* is widely used in European social discourse: it denotes a state of economic precariousness, where individuals live one small financial catastrophe away from homelessness.

For many on the Right, it would appear that this is the preferred way, or perhaps the only way thought possible. As the recent pandemic brought home to us all, however, we *need* general service workers. If everyone were an engineer, lawyer or mid-level manager, who would stock the warehouse shelves at Walmart? And to ask an entire class of much-needed fellow citizens to live in precarity and desperation, though working full-time every week to help meet the needs of the rest of us is, in my view, inhumane and immoral, and therefore not an option. What's more, I am convinced that if we practice the social democratic values of justice, solidarity and inclusion, and build a human capital culture, we will outproduce any economy based on fear and deprivation.

Worker Representation and Unions

A key component of a mature social democracy is *worker representation*. But before getting into some nuts and bolts, let's consider the philosophical argument for worker representation in a social democratic polity.

Social democracy, as we have shown, provides for an economy in which private citizens are permitted—in fact, encouraged—to acquire capital in order to form economic enterprises. This results in a society in which some individuals are owners of what Marx called the "means of production" while others are hired hands, employed to work in these enterprises for a salary or wages. Since the owners of the means of production are in charge of the enterprises they create, they have a tremendous amount of power over the individuals who work in them. Absent countervailing forces (such as trade unions and/or government regulation), owners are in control of both the wages and the working conditions of employees. The horrid conditions of workers in 19th-century industrial factories, sweat shops or coal mines (to mention a few examples among many), with 12-hour days for poverty wages in dangerous and unhealthy conditions, has shown us where this imbalance of power leads.

Unions were created, by workers everywhere in the industrialized world, as a means to gain some say over their compensation and work conditions. Their success in doing this is evidenced by the 40-hour work week, the prohibition of child labor, paid vacations, sick leave and many other workplace rules that, though we take them for granted today, were the result of hard struggles by union operatives and those they served to secure better lives for the majority of Americans. These associations of workers are not, as some on the right would argue, out-of-place interlopers in a market economy, but an element essential to the proper functioning of any society which allows the means of production to be controlled by private individuals.

If we take a broad view of the Commons we must see that, in some sense at least, the entire nation belongs to every citizen. For one thing, everyone within the political boundaries of the nation is asked to participate in the national project by following the laws promulgated by our various legislative bodies. Secondly, if the territorial integrity—or mere national interests—of the nation are threatened from without, all able-bodied males are called upon, through conscription, to risk their lives to defend it.[11] And as we have seen in past wars, the majority of those risking their lives on the front lines have been hired workers, not the "owners" of the nation's income-producing property.

So all are called upon to support the nation's institutions and defend its borders and interests, yet only a minority hold ownership of the "means of production," with all the powers that entails. Absent institutions to correct this imbalance, the working majority, who are co-owners of the nation-as-a-whole, would be left without any say in what is probably the most critical area of their lives: making a living. This would be both patently unfair and out of balance.

There are two major ways to correct this imbalance, in a

---

11. As of this writing, men (only) ages 18-25 must register with Selective Service. This could very possibly change to include women if a draft were ever again instituted.

private-enterprise economy, between owners and workers. One is through government regulation that takes into account the interests of workers in their workplaces. The other is through unions. Social democrats support both methods, as each has its own strengths and separate field of operation. Government can best make rules involving broad principles that should apply to every worker, such as the 40-hour workweek, minimum wages or safety precautions. Unions, on the other hand, are better positioned to exert influence on matters specific to the workers they represent: wage scales in a particular industry, work practices and the adoption of new technologies, to name a few.

Worker representation is one of several areas in which the United States shows itself to be a laggard in the development of social democracy. Among OECD nations, the United States, with one of its two major political parties opposed in principle to organized labor, is a rare outlier. Not even governments which are considered to be right of center in Europe, such as that of Emmanuel Macron in France, or of recently retired Angela Merkel in Germany, would ever propose eliminating unions, or suggest that they are a nefarious force in society which must be neutralized. These European leaders instead consider unions to be critical social partners and valued participants in the national dialogue. Nowhere among Europe's advanced economies do we find so-called "right-to-work laws," such as now exist in 28 American states, or other such hindrances to worker organization and representation. (The leaders of a large national union my own business used to work with preferred to call these laws "right to work for less" laws.)

To give an indication of how organized workers might be integrated into a national project, with broad support across all sectors of society, let's consider the case of Germany. Germany gained the world's admiration by the success with which it weathered the global economic downturn of 2008, its unemployment rate reaching a peak of 8 percent in 2009 and dropping rapidly to 6 percent by 2011 (in the U.S., unemployment reached 10 percent in 2009 and did not reach 6 percent again until the middle of 2014). Much of Germany's resilience during the global downturn, along with its remarkable success in maintaining a thriving manufacturing sector in the face of globalization, has been attributed by many specialists to its broadly supported system of worker representation.

Germany possesses a two-tiered system of worker representation. On the macro level there are numerous large unions, and most of them are members of DGB, a national federation which coordinates the activities of its member unions and speaks for unionized labor as a whole (an American analogy to the DGB would be the AFL-CIO). These unions operate much as do traditional unions in the United States, organizing workers and engaging in collective bargaining for their members. Their status is far greater in Germany, however, than is that of their American counterparts, and a far larger percentage of German workers than American are both union members and covered by union contracts.[12]

Another thing that distinguishes the German system from the American on the macro level is that German *employers* are also highly organized. The large majority of German firms are members of employer associations, organized by region and sector, and these associations participate in the Confederation of German Employer Associations. All engage in collective bargaining with trade unions, setting national, regional and sectoral standards.

If we turn to the micro level of German labor relations we find an institution with which Americans are generally not familiar—bodies called work councils. Under the provisions of a law promulgated in 1952 and revised in 1972, workers in

---

12. Sources differ, but it would appear that about half of German workers are covered by collective bargaining agreements as compared to only about 10% of American workers: https://economics. mit.edu/sites/default/files/publications/JEP_German_Model_of_ Industrial_Relations_Primer.pdf; https://www.bls.gov/news.release/ pdf/union2.pdf

every workplace in Germany with more than five employees are entitled to elect a work council.

German work councils "enjoy rights at a plant level that would make American managers shudder," writes Kathleen Thelan in *Union of Parts: Labor Politics in Postwar Germany.* Where work councils have the greatest power, in the steel and coal industries, workers' representatives enjoy parity with management on company supervisory boards as well as representation on the firm's board of directors, while the plant's local labor director represents both management and labor. According to Thelan, "virtually nothing happens in the steel industry without labor's assent." Even in other sectors, where the statutory powers of work councils are less extensive, management must acquire the approval of work councils for such routine plant decisions as "overtime, shift work, and wage and payment systems." Even in those areas where work council approval is not needed, management has a duty to keep workers' plant representatives informed of any changes which might affect employees. This allows union leaders not only to plan for any envisioned changes, but also to formulate strategies to mitigate possible adverse effects of those proposed changes.

One might think, given the powers granted work councils by German law, that German employers would not be fans of what is often referred to as "co-determination." This has not, however, been the case. "Employers have come to terms with co-determination," Thelan writes, "because it does not impede their ability to run capitalist companies successfully." By bringing employees' representatives into the decision-making processes at the plant level, work councils keep communication channels open. Instead of waiting for issues to reach the boiling point, where resort is had to strikes and other drastic measures, co-determination allows issues to be worked out as they come up, producing "ongoing compromise." Both sides know what they are dealing with, and employers "gain more predictability in plant operations." Many employers, Thelan writes, "acknowledge that the voice co-determination provides to employees has deepened loyalty to their firms, which in turn has enhanced company performance . . . . Co-determination," she continues, "has intertwined labor and management, tilting the incentive structure . . . toward social partnership and away from confrontation."

The benefits of Germany's co-determination model have been illustrated in how German firms have successfully confronted our increasingly globalized economy, allowing Germany to maintain a more solid manufacturing and export base than other advanced economies. With the comprehensive information about the firm's operations which, by law, workers' representatives are entitled to, they are in a position to understand the challenges faced by firms facing global competition. Speaking of the steel industry, Thelan writes: "Labor representatives and managers . . . largely agree on the problems the industry faces. Neither side, by and large, blames the other," and "both sides also largely concur on what German industry has to do to compete." When both sides can agree that some cost-cutting is the only way to save a company in the face of overseas competition, work councils allow input—and, importantly, buy-in—by labor's representatives. In German industry, these negotiated deals have typically involved early retirements with generous buy-outs, worker transfers to other plants and agreements by workers to work fewer hours, for marginally less pay, in order to keep more people employed. These strategies have helped keep German industry strong, kept workers in good jobs, and they helped Germany weather the 2008 recession with lower unemployment than other advanced economies.

None of this is to say that everything is hearts and flowers between German employers and their employees, nor that the national unions never need call a strike when agreement cannot be reached. But the German "dual-system" of "co-determination," codified in German laws, creates incentives for a more productive relationship between management and labor. If work councils' demands are too extreme, they will be resisted by management. Meanwhile, management is incentivized to work with labor's *reasonable* demands, because at the next work council election a more radical set of representatives may be chosen.

I would not suggest that any other country's system of labor relations could or should be directly transferred to the United States. We have our own unique history and a complicated federal system which requires tailored solutions. I would argue, however, that we have much to learn from Germany's system of worker representation. Work councils, in one form or another, are a feature of a number of social democratic nations in Europe, where the right of workers to have a say in the conditions of their work lives is taken for granted. The success of German manufacturing and export industries speaks to the fact that worker representation in company decisions is not only a win for employees, but also for employers and the nation as a whole.

Towards a Thirty-Hour Work Week

In the early industrial era many Americans worked atrocious hours, typically 10 to 12 hours a day for six days a week in factories and sweatshops, in mines and on railroads. A major focus of the first labor organizations in the 19th Century was the demand for a shorter work day. Through union strikes, bargaining and agitation, various sectors of the economy moved gradually toward shorter work days, and by the dawn of the 20th Century an 8-hour day had been achieved in various sectors of the economy. Ford Motors moved to an 8-hour day in 1914, and in 1916 a federal law codified an 8-hour day for railway workers throughout the country. It was not until the New Deal, however, and the passage of the National Labor Relations Act (1938, amended 1940), that employers were required to pay overtime to rank-and-file employees working more than 40 hours per week. In spite of the decreasing number of hours worked, American workers could produce so much more per hour, due to the increasing automation of work processes, that the nation's output continued to grow and its prosperity increase.

According to the U.S. Bureau of Labor Statistics, the productivity of American workers (the amount of stuff they can produce in a given amount of time) increased from 1947 to 2018 at an average rate of 2.1% per year. By a rough, simple calculation, then, American workers now produce, per hour worked, *4.3 times* more goods and services than they did in 1947. Yet they are still working a 40-hour week. And not only are workers still working 40 hours per week, but many more households have two workers than was the case in 1947.[13]

Part of the explanation for this is that we have more stuff than we did in 1947, including a lot of stuff that didn't then exist like cell phones, computers and the like. We have better and safer cars, larger houses and many more appliances, gadgets and personal services. But another part of the explanation lies in the fact that workers, as a whole, are receiving a smaller percentage of the nation's output as compared to owners. In fact, the share of the non-farm economic output of the nation accruing to workers, according the U.S. Bureau of Labor statistics, has decreased from around 66% in 1947 to around 58% today.[14]

I believe it is time to once again consider a shortening of the American work week. Many, many Americas, once they have put in their work shift and sat through long commutes, have virtually no time left for exercise and other forms of self-care, self-improvement or continuing education, social life and leisure, community involvement or child care and supervision. When both parents must work full time to get to the end of the month, many important elements of life—and most particularly attending to the needs of children—can go by the wayside. As a nation we are harried, distracted and disconnected from our communities; and our children are

---

13. https://www.bls.gov/productivity/
14. [https://www.bls.gov/opub/mlr/2017/article/estimating-the-us-labor-share.htm]

suffering unprecedented levels of anxiety and depression.

In our social democratic future, the average American worker will likely work a more humane 30-hour work week.[15] This makes sense from many angles. First, consider that two years after Ford Motors reduced its workforce's hours from nine to eight per day in 1914, the company's annual profit margin had grown from 30 million to 60 million dollars: in other words, the company's success skyrocketed! Rested, clear-thinking and happy employees do better work; are more likely to come up with innovative solutions to daily problems; are absent and ill less often; are less likely to quit, leading to expensive and disruptive recruiting and training; and the happy morale they spread throughout an enterprise provides a synergy that cannot be counted in dollars but is nonetheless invaluable. Much of the average 8-hour day is often wasted in any case, with an hour often spent at lunch and considerable unofficial dawdling.

A second positive effect of a shorter work week will be the creation of more jobs (as each worker will be working fewer hours), thus helping the nation sustain full employment.

Finally, a 30-hour week could go a long way toward handling the nation's childcare crisis. Consider two parents each working a six-hour day five days per week. Let's say their children go to school from 7:00 a.m. until 2:30 p.m. each day. With the parents working from 8:00 until 2:00 every day, *both parents* would be available, every day, to transport and supervise children during all non-school hours. If necessary, the parents could stagger their shifts so that one would be available in the morning and the other in the afternoon. I will leave it to economists to do the calculations, but the savings in childcare costs alone would be enormous. The improvement in the well-being of children (and thus in the effectiveness of

---

15. Like all measures proposed in this volume, the move toward a 30-hour workweek would be undertaken incrementally, reducing one hour every five years, for example, to allow businesses to adjust and to monitor for the measure's effect on such factors as overall productivity, inflation and employment levels.

America's future workforce) would be incalculable, the effect on the life of the average worker transformative. And it is my contention that overall productivity, if it changed at all, would go up.

Paid Leave

According to current statistics from the Bureau of Labor Statistics, about one-quarter of all U.S. workers receive no paid vacation or sick leave, a figure which rises to 46 percent for workers with earnings in the lowest decile (it really does flow downhill). In our social democratic future, all workers will be entitled to at least 20 days per year of paid vacation and sick leave.[16]

Wage Inequality in our Social Democratic Future

Inequality of both income and wealth has, in recent years, become a prominent topic in our national discourse, often tied in with identity politics claims by racialized groups and (self-proclaimed) advocates for women. In later sections I will address *wealth* inequality, as well as identity politics. Here I will limit myself to some general thoughts on *income* (as opposed to wealth) inequality in a social democratic future.

We'll begin with a tale from long ago. It is an apocryphal one, to be sure, but pertinent for our purposes. In this long-ago time, before the advent of our modern machines and cars and phones, there was a Kingdom ruled by a wise and benevolent Queen. The Kingdom possessed a mild climate and an abundance of good cropland, forest, game and water resources. For these reasons, and because of the wise and benevolent leadership of their Queen, the People were about as happy as people are capable of being.

Running through the very middle of the Kingdom, essentially dividing it in half, was a swift and deep river. In times even more ancient than those of our Kingdom, another civilization had built a sturdy stone bridge across the river,

16. https://www.huffpost.com/entry/low-wage-workers-least-like-ly-to-get-paid-holidays-and-vacation_n_66830695e4b038babc7c81c0

and since time immemorial the people of the Kingdom used that bridge to travel from one shore to the other. But then one day, under the pressure of a spring flood of extraordinary force, the ancient bridge collapsed. What's worse, the people of the Kingdom, having lost the engineering skills of the former civilization, were unable to replace the structure. Citizens were now forced to cross in primitive ferries which were really no more than shaky rafts. And because the river was deep and wide, with powerful, swiftly moving currents, many citizens of the Kingdom died while attempting to cross. Commerce was disrupted and many were those who, for fear of the dangerous current, found themselves cruelly separated from friends and family, or even the ability to make a living.

The compassionate Queen felt deeply for the trials her people were undergoing, and she thought hard and long upon the problem of the bridge. After several weeks of this cogitation, she appeared on one of the balconies of her castle, the balcony from which she was wont to make public pronouncements. When the People had gathered around, she said the following: "Since the tremendous flood I have been aware of the trials our people have undergone at the river. Many have drowned, and others, afraid to attempt the crossing, find themselves separated from near and dear. Many are those, I am told, who are unable to carry on their livelihoods as before. In order that we might regain our former peace and happiness, then, I hereby announce that any citizen who can build a new bridge across the river will be granted, as a token of our appreciation, five acres of our best cropland, with a stately home built by their fellow citizens, and ten gold florins to boot!"

There were oohs and aahs among the crowd, because in that long-ago Kingdom, to possess five acres was quite something, to possess a stately home was nearly unheard of, and ten gold florins to boot! They looked around at one another, but in no one's eyes did anyone detect a spark that might suggest any clue as to how such a bridge might be built.

But in a distant village lived a young man who was not at the Castle that day. He had always been a little different than the other boys of the village. While they played at games, or lazed summer afternoons away lounging in the meadow swapping stories of doubtful veracity, he busied himself, using sticks, stones and even his mother's dishes, building miniature structures in the little yard behind his family's cottage. He had built a replica of the Queen's castle (based upon travelers' reports, for he had surely never journeyed to the Kingdom's capital!) and small ox carts with real wheels that rolled. Once he even built a bridge of sticks and stones across a tiny rivulet that ran through the yard after the spring rains. Being of a curious nature, he had also made the acquaintance of the friars at the nearby abbey. Noting his interest in learning, one of the kindest of the churchmen taught him to read and allowed him to browse in the abbey's library. Though the collection was laughably small by modern standards, there were a couple of books about mathematics and even a dusty volume, translated from the ancient Greek, on engineering principles. These books became favorites of the boy, and when he was not helping his family with farm work and other chores, he slipped away to the library to spend his hours with the friars' books. The other boys, and also many of the girls, teased him. They even came up with a taunting nickname: the "Scholar."

After he grew into manhood, the Scholar had less time to spend at the abbey, for he had married, fathered two children, and now spent his days tending to his family's crops, animals, tools and buildings. But he never forgot the ancient knowledge he had read in the friars' books, and not only his family but the entire village benefited. His cottage and outbuildings were the sturdiest in the village, thanks to improvements he had made, and he spearheaded the diversion of a nearby stream and the building of an irrigation system for the villagers' crops. Though his neighbors still felt him somewhat odd, the nickname "Scholar" was now not so much a taunt as a mark of respect.

It took three weeks, in those slower times, for news of the Queen's pronouncement about the bridge to reach the Scholar's village. But when it did, we can imagine its effect upon the imagination of the young man. Recalling the small-scale projects he had built as a boy, and the mathematical and engineering principles he had studied in the friars' books he began, as he worked in the fields by day, and also while he sat by firelight in his family's cottage at night, to picture how a bridge might be built over the raging river. After several weeks of this intense thought he began to make drawings and then, in his rare free hours, to build small replicas in the cottage yard.

I think you know where this story is going, and how it ends. The young man travels to the Castle, where he presents the Queen with his schematics and his model. She okays the effort, placing all needed resources at the Scholar's disposal. The bridge is built and successfully withstands the river's current. The Scholar is rewarded with five acres of good cropland, a stately home and ten gold florins.

I have presented this tale, perhaps a little whimsical, with a serious purpose: to serve as a model for how we might think about income inequality in our social democratic future. Society has a problem it would like to solve. In our story, a bridge must be built. The Queen, the People's representative, suspects that there may be someone in the Kingdom who knows how to solve the problem of the bridge. But the question is, how to find that person, and how to instigate them to share their capacities with the Kingdom? Were the Queen aware of the existence of the Scholar, and that he might be able to build the bridge, she could conceivably have sent her soldiers to his village, kidnapped him and forced him, upon pain of torture, to manage the construction of such a bridge. There have been societies where, no doubt, such procedures have been used. We modern Americans, however, strongly frown upon kidnapping, torture and involuntary servitude, as did the wise and benevolent Queen. What's more, the performance of the Scholar under duress would almost certainly be inferior to what he might accomplish with a positive motivation.

The Queen, not only benevolent but wise in the ways of human nature, recognized that her best chance of finding someone to build the bridge lay in offering some personal incentive. And did the People, after the bridge was built, resent the fact that the Scholar lived in a bigger house, possessed five good acres and had ten gold florins to boot? I doubt it. Instead, they gave a friendly wave when they passed his stately home, remembering how the Scholar had saved their bacon. They may have even calculated—the Scholar's unusual life story having now become legend—that he had received no more than his just deserts. After all, while the other children were lazing about and taunting him with nicknames, wasn't he working away on his models or studying tedious texts at the abbey library? In other words, the Queen's offer of greater reward for the building of the bridge was not merely pragmatic, in that it offered the quickest and best solution to her problem, but it was also *just*. The Scholar had spent more of his time and effort accumulating skills and knowledge that would prove to be of great benefit to the Kingdom. Was it not right that he should receive some additional reward for his additional effort?

And so likewise in our social democratic future, we will not begrudge some extra reward for those who provide value, above and beyond the norm, to our communities and our nation. Such rewards serve everyone's interest, as they incentivize individuals both to improve their knowledge, skills and competencies and also to make extraordinary efforts. They are also just, inasmuch as they provide greater reward where greater effort has been exerted.

But what if the Queen, rather than rewarding the Scholar a statelier than average home, five acres and ten gold florins, had rewarded him with one-tenth of the Kingdom's lands, sixteen stately homes and so many gold florins that he would never have to work again? What if his wealth, invested at interest and ever growing, was soon on a par with the wealth of entire nations, and he was able to command vast quantities of the Kingdom's resources, with thousands of his fellow citizens now working to tend his lands, clean his many homes, and transport him around the Kingdom in a golden palanquin so that he might show off his elevated status? The once humble Scholar has now taken on something of an attitude: It seems that he now believes that his exalted self deserves every resource he can get his hands on. Not only that, but with the great wealth he now possesses he has purchased followers and armed private retainers. Soon, in fact, he is threatening the authority of the very Queen who made his rise possible.

At this point, as you might imagine, the People no longer smile gratefully when they pass the Scholar's home or when they see him parading around the Kingdom in his golden palanquin, surrounded by lackeys. Nor do they enjoy seeing his lazy children gallivanting around with their noses in the air, commanding the labor of them and their honest, hard-working neighbors with arrogance, although not a one of them has ever contributed so much as one ounce of energy to the Kingdom's prosperity. The People do not necessarily resent the Scholar's good fortune, for the People of the Kingdom are a good people, not given to pettiness. But while they still appreciate the building of the bridge, they find it hard to understand why the Scholar's one beneficent act on behalf of his fellow citizens has entitled him to a life of ongoing luxury and the capacity to command, for his personal benefit, such a huge proportion of the resources which they produce (they find it even harder to comprehend why his children, who have never done anything for the good of the People, enjoy the same emoluments). As for his ability, with his army of private retainers, to exert pressure on the just and benevolent Queen regarding the decisions she makes on behalf of her people, they are deeply concerned.

And so likewise, while we will look with favor, in our social democratic future, upon allowing individuals who produce benefits above and beyond the norm to receive rewards above and beyond the norm, there will be limits! Too much income inequality is inimical to a truly social democratic future. Firstly, at its extremes, income inequality strikes most of us as patently *unjust,* as for example when CEO compensation rises to hundreds or even thousands of times the wages of the average worker in the enterprises they command. (While we readily recognize the greater knowledge, skills, experience and even dedication that have brought a CEO to a leadership position, it is hard to conceive that the value they add could be thousands of times that of the corporation's line-level workers.) Secondly, too much income inequality damages vital social democratic values. When some live like potentates, while others who work hard every day struggle in precarity, we can have neither *solidarity* nor *inclusion.* Different segments of society, so different in their relationship to material comfort and security, may as well be living on different planets. They will not understand one another's needs and struggles and, ultimately, will lose the ability to care about one another. Walls will be built, figurative as well as literal (think, for example, of gated communities) and the dream of unified communities and nation, where all are *included* and *solidarity* reigns, goes up in smoke. Those on the lower end of the income scale, like the citizens of our Kingdom, will not understand how it can possibly be just that, toiling away on a daily basis, they cannot achieve what most of their fellows would consider a dignified existence while others, like the Scholar, are exorbitantly rewarded. This leads to alienation, apathy about society and the weakening of the social contract, with the attendant criminality and other anti-social behaviors that flow from a lack of *inclusion* and *solidarity.* Thirdly, extreme inequality of *income* leads almost inevitably to even greater inequalities of *wealth.* Due to the way that money works in our current society, once one acquires a certain amount above and beyond one's fellow citizens one is likely to acquire always more and more (through investments in appreciating assets) until the difference becomes astronomical. These great fortunes are typically passed on to their creators' descendants and heirs, fostering something inimical not only to our social democratic dream but also the very founding principles of the American Republic: inter-generational aristocracies such as those that our nation's founders were determined to leave behind in Europe. And because these fortunes are frequently used to fund political causes (e.g., Koch brothers), these dynasties of wealth become also dynasties of *power*, perverting a cardinal principle of our social democratic future: that every voting citizen should wield an equal say in how our communities, states and nation are organized.

The question, then, becomes the following: "How do we allow inequality of income sufficient to incentivize people to acquire skills and knowledge, and to work harder and smarter, while not allowing such inequality to become so great that it strikes us as *unjust*, damages *solidarity* and *inclusion*, and leads to inequalities of wealth which pervert our American system by creating inter-generational aristocracies of wealth and power?" This question will be dealt with in detail in later sections, when we look at the *Commons*, inheritance, rentier[17] income and taxation, but at this juncture I will stipulate, first, that the system of living wages for willing workers already described in these pages will go a good way toward compressing the income spread in our society. Second, *income* will be taxed more progressively in order to finance the *just* and *humane* society we construct, further reducing (after-tax) income inequality. Third, we will tax accumulated wealth. Finally, through a proper conception of what constitutes the *Commons*, and the capturing of *rentier* income, the accumulation of such absurdly large fortunes as those commanded by Bill Gates or Jeff Bezos will be impossible.

Make no mistake, we would not wish to disincentive a

---

17. Income derived not from productive effort but from owning things, such as that made through appreciation of assets or collecting rents.

future Bill Gates or Jeff Bezos from developing enterprises that greatly benefit all of us. Who doesn't find Microsoft Word easier than our old typewriters; and who doesn't appreciate finding that sought-after item on Amazon? But if we put ourselves in the position of the Queen in our Kingdom, we must ask ourselves how much incentive we must offer in order to obtain the desired benefit (in her case, the building of the bridge)? As we saw, the Scholar was willing to build the bridge for five acres, one stately home and ten gold florins. I would argue likewise that Gates and Bezos would have founded and elaborated the enterprises for which they are famous for far less than the over-one-hundred billions in fortunes they have each now acquired. I would argue, in fact, that if each of them had been told, when they were young men starting out, that they might achieve lifetime fortunes of one hundred million dollars each if they could, respectively, create a computerized word processing program or an online shopping network, they would have worked just as hard as they did. In other words, the Queen needn't offer one-tenth of the Kingdom's lands, sixteen stately homes and thousands of gold florins when five acres, one stately home and ten gold florins is enough. In handing over control over such huge quantities of our economy's output to plutocrats like Gates and Bezos we have given away the proverbial store. We have struck a bad bargain, for we certainly could have achieved the benefit they provided for far less. We may have been a *benevolent* Queen, but we have not been a very *wise* one. And in *over*-rewarding these entrepreneurs, helpful individuals to whom, granted, we should be grateful for their contributions, we have been *unjust* to those who are *under*-compensated for working hard every day. We have damaged *solidarity* and *inclusion,* and we have put too much power into the hands of private individuals, thus perverting true democracy. Further, we have enabled the likely creation of inter-generational *dynasties of wealth and power* which are inimical to the fundamental principles of this American Republic.

Nuts & Bolts:

Nurturing the Young

There is no more important task for any human community than nurturing the young. If we consider a society's ongoing future, it is axiomatic that the adults who, tomorrow, will maintain necessary functions and uphold our values and institutions are the children of today. If we want tomorrow's society to be strong and functional, we must ensure that today's children and young people develop their full potentials for contributing to the common welfare, and also that they internalize a commitment to the well-being of their communities, their nation and their fellow citizens.

Let's consider these issues, for a moment, in light of the social democratic values we have established. First, social democrats believe in a society which is both *just* and *humane*. A society in which some children have comprehensive pre-school education, copious enrichment activities, special tutors, elite private schools and test-preparation classes, while others do not, is not a *just* society. Nor is a society in which some children, by accident of birth, are sentenced to undeveloped potentials and marginalization a society which is *humane*. Neglect toward the young also works against the social democratic value of *inclusion* and damages *solidarity*. The marginalized child not only suffers the injury of undeveloped potential and marginalization, but such a child, perceiving that society is neither *just* nor *humane*, is unlikely to develop a commitment to that society's values, institutions, or to the well-being of fellow citizens. Such a child, excluded and lacking feelings of *solidarity*, is more likely than others to become a burden on society: to require assistance from the state, turn to substance abuse, or exhibit criminal and other anti-social behavior. The money we think we are saving by failing to provide for the child's needs when young we are likely to spend later in state assistance, mental health support, substance addiction remediation or in the criminal justice and prison system.

Conservatives typically advocate for rewards based upon merit and regularly advance this argument as a claim against social assistance programs, minimum wages and other state interventions. (They appear to have no problem, however, with certain individuals gaining wealth without any show of merit: for example, through inheritance or through the appreciation of passive assets; nor do they object to massive subsidies for agricultural and certain industrial sectors.) Social democrats also believe in reward for merit. But the idea of a merit-based system can have little meaning without the parallel idea of a level playing field. To give some children every advantage while leaving others marginalized, their potentials undeveloped, and then to say that some will receive far greater rewards, as adults, on account of a greater display of merit, is perverse. In marginalizing one group of children we have predestined that they will have less merit when they are adults, where "merit" is defined as the possession of education and skills, including social skills, that are valued in the marketplace.

Some will argue that society cannot completely "level the playing field" for children, since the success of a child's upbringing depends to a large extent upon the quality of parenting the child receives. And it is no doubt true that a child with negligent, abusive, socially disconnected, mentally ill, uneducated or anti-social parents (or parent) will be less likely to develop potentials and succeed in society than a child whose parents are attentive, caring, socially connected, psychologically well-adjusted, educated and socially responsible. (Studies also indicate that children with two parents in the home, in the aggregate, do better on common success metrics than children raised in single-parent homes.) And I would agree that, unless we are to have all children raised by identical androids, we will not be able to eradicate disparities in the quality of parenting children receive. We can, however, endeavor to create a social democratic society in which there will be fewer negligent, abusive, socially disconnected, mentally ill, uneducated and anti-social parents. We can also do our best to help those children whose family backgrounds fall short of parenting ideals.

A further objection, sure to be advanced by some, is that any attempt to level life's playing field is a fool's errand because "life isn't fair." This old saw is partly true. There are things about life that convey advantages or disadvantages, even apart from the parents we are born to—such as how tall or strong we are, whether we are considered good-looking, our susceptibility to disease conditions or our intellectual potential—which cannot be changed. But when we refuse to change things that can be changed to make life more fair, it is not *life* that isn't fair. It is our choices, and our society, which are not fair.

And there are things that we *can* change.

In our social democratic future, the collective, working through government, will—to the greatest extent possible—level the playing field for all children by equalizing educational and other developmental opportunities. Some children's parents will be able, on their own, to provide everything they need to fully develop their potentials. For those whose parents cannot, however, the state will do everything possible to make sure that no child's potentials go undeveloped and that no child is marginalized. We will know we have succeeded at this task when we can look any child, from any household, in the eyes and honestly say: "Your chances of fully developing your potentials as a human being, and of fully participating in the social, cultural, economic and political life of your community and nation are equal to those of any other child in this nation, from any household, in any zip code."

Nurturing the Young: Quality Public Education

So how will a social democratic America support children and the young, equalizing chances to the greatest extent possible? One pillar of this process is already in place: the public school system. But it must be improved. All children, in every state, must have access to a free, world-class education, of comparable quality across zip codes from pre-school through the secondary grades. College, for those who demonstrate the aptitude for higher learning, will be affordable though a mix of parental income, loans and grants. Universal, quality pre-K will itself go a long way toward closing the reading gap, on account of which more-advantaged children enter the first grade already reading while others may have seldom seen a book.

Nurturing the Young: After School Centers

Since much of a child's development takes place outside of school, our future social democracy must also consider what goes on in a child's non-school hours. More-advantaged children participate in myriad extra-curricular activities, from sports to music lessons. The most economically advantaged often have one parent always at home, making sure homework is done and rendering assistance as necessary. Children from the most challenging environments go home to a neighborhood rife with crime and drugs, with no parent present, and are left to their own devices—if not exploitation by bad actors. To provide for these children, and all others who wish to participate, every school in our social democratic future will double as an after-school center. Such centers, of course, already exist, and do a great deal of good. The after-school centers of our social democratic future, however, will differ in two ways from currently existing centers. They will be universal (at every school) and they will offer a far more comprehensive array of services than today's units. They will also remain open and fully functioning during school breaks: including summer vacation.

These centers will, at the most basic level, provide a safe, adult-supervised environment for kids. But they will also be centers of enrichment. Each center will be staffed, first, with tutors (these could be teachers working overtime, student teachers from local colleges, volunteers from higher grades, professional tutors, or a mix) to see that children finish homework, providing any needed help. There will be athletic programs, music and art lessons, and spaces for recreation: after homework is done, of course. Center staff could coordinate participation with extra-curricular activities already offered by the school. Child psychologists, traveling between centers, will be available to help with adjustment problems. These centers will stay open throughout the evening, providing kids with a space to grow, develop and recreate that may not be available at home.

Nurturing the Young: Career Formation and the German Model

As children transition into adolescence and advance through their teen years, we must begin to contemplate their eventual integration into the adult world. Keeping the centrality of work in mind, in our social democratic future we will accompany the student on the journey of finding an appropriate career. Under the current American system, too many young adults are dumped out of high school with no job skills and no plan for acquiring them. Let us consider, for a moment, the very different German education system.

The German education system offers several different instructional paths, based upon a student's aptitudes and interests, and designed to maximize their readiness to join the adult world of work once their formal education is completed.

Between the ages of six and ten (grades 1 through 4), all German students attend the same type of elementary school. After that, however, students (and their parents) select among several types of *lower-secondary* school. The lower-secondary schools, depending on the type, run from the 5th through the 9th or 10th grades. (School attendance is compulsory for nine to ten years in Germany, depending on the state.)

Only about one-third of German students choose *Gymnasia* schools—demanding academic institutions specifically geared toward eventual enrollment at a university—at the lower-secondary level. Most of the remaining two-thirds of German students choose between two other types of lower secondary schools, the *Hauptschule* or the *Realschule*.

Though the least academically oriented of the schooling tracks, *Hauptschule* programs still require students to master a thorough general education, with courses in German, math and English compulsory in most German states; and completion of *Hauptschule* satisfies Germany's compulsory education requirement. (*Hauptschule* students also study such standard secondary subjects as natural and social sciences, arts and music.) The *Hauptschule* is geared, generally speaking, toward those who anticipate entering the manual trades. After 9th Grade, *Hauptschule* students take an examination in order to receive a certificate of completion, the *Zeugnis des Hauptschulabschlusses* (certificate of completion of Hauptschule). This certificate qualifies the student to move on to targeted vocational training in the upper secondary (high school) years.

Realschule schools, like *Hauptschules*, satisfy Germany's compulsory education requirement, but the curriculum is more demanding than in *Hauptschules*, and programs run through the 10th rather than 9th grade. After successfully completing final exams, students in the *Realschule* program receive the *Zeugnis des Realschulabschlusses* (certificate of completion of Realschule). Like the *Hauptschule* certificate, successful completion of *Realschule* qualifies the student to move on to upper secondary vocational training. But there are more options for *Realschule* graduates, including white collar career tracks such as hotel management and accounting. In addition, *Realschule* graduates may transfer to the university oriented track, the

Gymnasia, though this may depend, in some German states, on their grades in key subjects.

Most students, after completing either *Realschule* or *Hauptschule,* move into upper secondary vocational training. Germany's vocational system, admired throughout the world, prepares students who will not attend university for real careers with decent wages. And Germany's youth unemployment rate—at 5.8% pre-pandemic and only 7.5% in 2020, the lowest in Europe and the envy of other OECD nations—is generally credited to the country's vocational education tracks.[1] German students in upper-secondary vocational programs study everything from auto mechanics and carpentry to business, banking and information systems (with, as noted, a *Hauptschule* certificate generally required for training programs in manual trades and the *Realschule* required for white collar fields). About two-thirds of classroom time is occupied with targeted instruction in the chosen field, while the other third is devoted to a continuation of general education courses begun in lower secondary school.

Key to the success of Germany's vocational programs is the real-world experience afforded students who choose these educational tracks. More than three quarters of German students enrolled in upper-secondary vocational programs split their time between classroom instruction and real workplace experience with participating companies. These young people represent nearly half of all secondary school students in Germany.

Some students in this "dual" system spend a certain number of days per week at a workplace and the others in class. Others alternate blocks of several weeks of classroom instruction with weeks-long blocks in a real-world work environment. There are no formal admission requirements for the dual-track programs. Participating companies set their own

1. The U.S. youth unemployment rate has run between 8 and 18 percent in the 21st Century, and reached over 20% in 2020.; https://www.iab-forum.de/en/youth-unemployment-in-germany-and-the-united-kingdom-in-times-of-covid-19/

standards, and they are not required to accept any student. It is possible, though not common, for students without the standard lower secondary certificates to enter vocational programs, and in some cases, graduates of the university oriented *Gymnasia* program pursue vocational training. Participating companies' training programs must meet national standards, and the employers are required to pay student trainees a modest salary.

Upon completion of the classroom component, dual-system students receive the *Abschlusszeugnis der Berufsschule*, or certificate of completion of vocational training. Students are normally required to take final exams, which test both their theoretical and practical knowledge. These tests are developed by state bodies, but also by professional associations (lawyers, doctors), Chambers of Crafts, and Chambers of Industry and Commerce. In all, there are 325 officially recognized vocational qualifications, with their corresponding tests, in every field from dental tech to film editor.

As might have been inferred, Germany's upper secondary vocational programs train students for many occupations that normally require a college degree in the United States. Most students, upon completing vocational programs at roughly the age of eighteen, are prepared to begin a career for which they have received extensive training, and for which they can expect to be paid a decent wage.

The roughly one-third of German students who do not follow the vocational track through *Hauptschule* and *Realschule* in the lower secondary grades (grades five through nine or ten), with a dual-vocational program in the upper secondary grades (grades ten or eleven through twelve) follow the university oriented *Gymnasia* program. University education, as is true across much of Europe, is largely reserved for those pursuing careers in the learned professions (law, medicine), teaching or executive positions in government and industry. The curricula in the *Gymnasia* schools is more academically rigorous than in the *Hauptschules* and *Realschules* (a second foreign language is required beginning in lower secondary grades, for example) and students are expected to learn more independently in preparation for the university experience.

As has been noted, the German educational system is admired around the world, and it is often credited with contributing to both Germany's low youth unemployment rate and to its world class economy—one of the few which has been able to maintain a strong manufacturing base in the face of global competition. The system has also had its critics, however, including within Germany itself, the main complaint being that it pigeon-holes students at too early an age, foreclosing options they might wish to pursue later. Germany has responded to these critiques, over the last several decades, by adding more flexibility to the system. Students may now switch, for example, from the *Realschule* into the university oriented *Gymnasia* in midstream, or in some cases go into university directly from a *Realschule*. Most German states have also developed "combination" or "comprehensive" schools, in which the more trades-oriented *Hauptschule* students study together with the more white collar oriented *Realschule* students, and where changing tracks is facilitated. In the last several years, responding perhaps to an economy which increasingly requires lifelong learning and technical expertise, enrollment in the *Hauptschules* has declined, while enrollment in the newer comprehensive schools has skyrocketed.

Most American high schools already offer vocational curricula, at varying degrees of comprehensiveness, though nowhere in the U.S. do we find vocational tracks as fully developed as in the German model. Transplanting a system such as Germany's to the United States would be no easy matter, nor would I recommend that we copy any system without taking into account American realities. The U.S. system, founded in American ideals of equality, has generally been resistant to attempts to separate students into completely separate schools at too early an age. Though tracking by ability within the same school is not uncommon, even this practice is a subject of hot debate, its critics claiming that it stigmatizes students tracked into less academic levels and can foster racial segregation.

These critiques are not easily dismissed, and I am all for the support of students' self-esteem and against the bunkering of students by racialized groupings. We must, however, confront a broken American education system which every year produces millions of eighteen-year-old adults who lack the qualifications, interest or aptitude for university education and have not been afforded any job skills with which to make a living beyond menial labor at low wages. (This is not to mention the further hundreds of thousands who, bored and seeing no purpose in their schooling, drop out before receiving a diploma.) We must ask whether these students' secondary education years might be best spent preparing them for a future career, with appropriate training and some real-world experience. Keeping students destined for manual trades or technical fields in "equal" tracks with university-bound students who must master the arts of scholarly research and higher mathematics does them no favors. Instead it wastes their precious time, along with an opportunity to give them the skills they will need to command their own destinies in the workplace. It could be argued that in today's America we have ended up with an educational system even more stratified, in practice, than Germany's. Students of well-off, well-educated parents have an education and career path laid out through private schools and top universities, with plenty of tutoring and test-taking classes along the way. Those not bound for college, meanwhile, are given little meaningful help in finding their way into decent employment.

Our social democratic future of work envisions employment and training Hubs, closely coordinated with our community college system. The U.S. should develop a German-like dual-system for upper secondary students destined for trades and technical fields, tied into this adult world of work and training. Our future social democracy, as I have already stipulated, will be founded on the continual development of *human capital,* and this development should begin at birth and continue seamlessly into and throughout adulthood. By ensuring that all adolescents and young adults, not just the college bound, have a viable career path ahead of them, we will remain true to the vital social democratic value of *inclusion.*

Nuts & Bolts:

The Commons

The Commons is a term not generally heard in American political discourse, but the concept it describes is a vital component in the social democratic worldview. The *Commons*, briefly put, encompasses all those things which belong not to private individuals but to everyone. There is no debate, as stated in this book's introduction, that this includes the air we breathe, major waterways or the aquifers we tap for drinking water. I will here propose several additional elements which, in our social democratic future, will be considered the common property of us all.

About Property

Before we decide which things are the property of individuals, and which the property of all, let's take a look at the concept of property itself. British philosopher David Hume (1711-1776) wrote that "the convention for the distinction of property, and for the stability of possession, is of all circumstances the most necessary to the establishment of human society." In other words Hume (along with several other philosophers of the Enlightenment era) decided that the determining and enforcing of *who owns what*, whether it be money in your bank account, agricultural fields, or your home and carriage, is the chief function of government. Knowing what we now know, thanks to the work of cultural anthropologists, about pre-state societies, and given the far greater number of functions of modern governments as compared to those of Hume's day, we might question, or wish to nuance, his premise. But no one would argue that the determination of *who owns what* remains at least one of the central, if not *the* central function of government. Little in our lives is more crucial to each of us than the knowledge that our homes, or our cars, or the money in our bank accounts is reserved for our own exclusive use, and that no one can mess with any of if without our permission.

We have already touched on another Enlightenment philosopher, one whose influence on the founding of the United States was incalculable, and that is John Locke (1632-1704). Locke preached that the ownership of property was a *natural* right. That is, he averred that the right to own private property is inherent in the very nature of human beings. Given these beliefs, it is not strange that he agreed with Hume that government's chief role is the protection of a citizen's right to own and hold their private property. Modern conservatives love John Locke, employing his conceptions of *natural man* to justify both the unlimited accumulation of wealth and resistance to taxation.

John Locke lived in an England in which the ownership of land was the key source of wealth. He predated the modern academic discipline of cultural anthropology and perhaps was unaware that many contemporaneous tribal peoples did not practice the private ownership of landed property. Instead, such groups typically lay claim to a common territory in which they hunt and forage and which they protect from other *groups*. What Locke saw as a *natural* right, the capacity of each individual to acquire and exclusively possess land, was rather a convention adopted by the society in which he lived at a given point in time and then imposed by successive governments. It was no coincidence that these governments, undemocratic and oligarchical, were controlled by an aristocracy which (you guessed it!) happened to own most of the land.

The organizers of the United States were profoundly influenced by Locke's ideas. It is also not a coincidence, in this regard, that they too were part of an aristocracy which monopolized an outsized portion of landed wealth in Britain's North American colonies, and that they created a Republic whose highly limited franchise guaranteed that those possessing landed wealth, and their progeny, would shape government policy going forward.

Without digressing further into historical antecedents, suffice to say that American political discourse has been shaped from the beginning by Locke's conception that it is *natural* (part of our nature as *homo sapiens*) for societies to divide up the territory they inhabit into separate parcels, and to give the exclusive right to use these parcels to separate individuals. And this right, going back to feudal times, is considered to be *eternal* and inter-generational. That is to say, the exclusive right to possess whatever property one acquires in one's lifetime is passed on to one's heirs, and then to their heirs, and so on in perpetuity.

As noted, modern conservatives love John Locke's conception of property possession as *natural* to our species, for it justifies not only the unrestricted accumulation of wealth but also resistance to its regulation or taxation. If the property I acquire (or inherit) is mine by *natural* right, what right has the government (a man-made convention) to take it away from me via the mechanism of taxation, to redistribute it, or to impose regulations upon its uses?

This line of reasoning, however, fails to recognize a critically important point. That is this: there is no such thing as property except inasmuch as *the government makes it so.* No, there is no *natural* imperative, part and parcel of being *homo sapiens*, that individuals possess property for their exclusive use, as the labors of cultural anthropologists have established. We possess property for exclusive use only because the government both (1) says that we do, and (2) ensures our right to possess it. The deed to your home or car lacks full legal effect until it is recorded at a *government* records office, and if a dispute arose with a neighbor about your boundary line, it would be settled by a court, another *government* function. If a band of criminals were then to appear at your property, telling you that they were moving in and you were moving out, you would call the police, yet another agency of the *government*. Without government, that is, we would each have exclusive use only of that property which we, along with allied relatives and friends, could defend against others who wished to take it away from us. Giving David Hume his due, it is the government that performs this central role, if not *the* central role, of deciding *who owns what*, not some natural right. Without government, we would live in lawless chaos, where each of our rights to possess anything would be at the mercy of the most aggressive, violent and unprincipled among us.

If I have taken pains to establish that it is the collective, acting through government, that decides *who owns what*, it is so that we might reconsider current conceptions of property rights in keeping with a more just and humane social democratic future, one founded on the ideals of solidarity and inclusion and compatible with a social democratic conception of human nature (that we are both an individual and a communal species). If we dismiss Locke's idea that the exclusive possession of property (chiefly land, in his era) is a *natural* right, inherent in the human condition, we are free to rethink which things should properly belong to private individuals and those which should remain part of the *Commons*, our collective inheritance.

Private Property

Let us begin this exploration of *who should own what* with the private side, encapsulated in the question, what things should rightly belong to private individuals for their exclusive use? I will first state a basic moral premise: private individuals should have the right to exclusively possess those things which they themselves are responsible for creating, or which they have duly purchased from someone else who was responsible for creating them. I did not create the sky, for example, and it would be absurd for me to claim that I own it—as it would be absurd for me to claim that I own the Pacific Ocean or the Potomac River. However, if I purchase several skeins of yarn and with them weave a rug, who would claim that anyone but me has a right to possess that rug? By similar logic, we can say that if Paul McCartney single-mindedly dreamt up the song "Yesterday" and then recorded it, the recording of that song is his property. He, and no one but him, created it. Were it not for Sir Paul, "Yesterday" would not exist. To take a couple of slightly more complicated examples, if a property developer organizes the resources to build an office tower, or an entrepreneur a factory, a social democrat would not challenge their right to the exclusive possession and essential control (without prejudice, of course, to the State's right to regulate and tax) of these enterprises. If it were not, after all, for the efforts of these individuals, these things would not exist either.

Scarce Resources

Let's now look at some things that no one created. In this category we have oil and other mineral reserves, forests (where they are not intentionally planted) and, for that matter, all naturally occurring resources, including any piece of land. Although these things were created by no one, but exist spontaneously as part of our environment, we allow individuals to exclusively possess them. We even allow individuals to pass these types of property onto their descendants or other heirs in perpetuity (yes, *forever*).

Let's say that I inherit 100 acres of land and it is later found to conceal substantial oil or other mineral reserves. Under our current system, these mineral reserves, like the land itself, are considered to be my private property. I can then require my fellow citizens to pay to me whatever price the "market will bear" in order to use these resources—resources which I had nothing to do with creating. I will likely become exorbitantly wealthy in the process, although I have made no productive contribution to my society's economy, thus making a mockery of our claims to be a society where rewards are based upon *merit*.

In our social democratic future we will look back upon such scenarios as backward and absurd. Why should private individuals be given the exclusive control over valuable mineral resources, the supply of which is limited and which they had nothing to do with creating (the credit for this goes to natural processes acting in deep geologic time), forcing the rest of us into a hard bargain in order to enjoy their use? In our more intelligent social democratic future, all such resources will be considered part of the *Commons*, part of our *national patrimony*. This will include not only mineral reserves but also forests, as well as the agricultural croplands now typically controlled by gigantic agribusinesses.

But how, you might ask, will these resources be exploited, if they are not owned by private individuals and businesses? The answer is that these resources will still be exploited by private parties, in keeping with the social democratic preference for a chiefly private-enterprise economy. These private parties will simply not *own* them. We already have a template for this system in the leases put out on federal government lands for everything from mining to forestry to grazing. The difference in our social democratic future is that all such resources will be in the ownership of the collective and managed by government. Government, acting on the collective's behalf, will offer resource-bearing lands for lease to enterprises organized to extract the resources they contain. Concessionaires will submit bids to explore and develop these resources, and government will drive the best possible bargain on behalf of the People. We might think back, here, to the analogy of the Queen and the Bridge. As did that Queen, the collective will offer rewards to energetic and ambitious parties willing to solve collective problems: in this case, mineral extraction, forestry, agriculture and the like. And like the wise Queen, we will not give more than is necessary to incentivize participation! Forces of supply and demand will determine the rents that private parties will pay the collective for the opportunity to extract and sell the resources on these *Commons.*

Placing such resources within the *Commons* will carry multiple advantages. First, government will manage these lands with an eye towards sustainability, climate stabilization and with the good of all in mind, considering not only our need for resources but also the value of wild places for recreation and spiritual and emotional health. Government will not face constant lawsuits about its right to regulate such lands for the common good as against the countervailing claims of private parties, for government, as the owner of the land, will have an unchallenged right to regulate its possessions as it sees fit.

Secondly, in placing such resources among the *Commons* we eliminate a chief source of *rentier income,* thereby making society fairer and more merit-based. The term *rentier income* refers to income which is earned through no effort on the part of the one who earns it: income which is gained simply by the fact of *owning* something. In its most pure form, rentier income is derived from owning things which no human being has created: for example, forested land from which timber is harvested, land on which shale oil deposits are discovered, or land once peripheral to an urban area which is suddenly worth tens of millions because a developer wishes to put an upscale residential subdivision or trendy mixed development on the site. A chief principle of our future social democracy will be to eliminate such pure rentier income wherever possible.[1]

As will be remembered, we aspire to a *just* society, one in which reward is truly based on *merit,* where one receives economic rewards in exchange for the creation of goods and services needed and wanted by one's fellow citizens. It is

---

1. We will look more closely at other forms of rentier income in a later section (stocks and bonds; landlordism; ownership of businesses): these will require more nuanced approach than income derived from the simple ownership and sale of natural resources.

patently unjust, and flies in the face of *merit,* to allow individuals to achieve economic gains without any contribution to our collective prosperity. *Solidarity* is damaged, perhaps fatally so, when some individuals receive exorbitant windfalls though making no contribution to our collective productive efforts, while others must struggle at their jobs day by day in order to get by. These latter perceive, and rightly so, that society is neither fair nor based on merit. Social discontent, disconnection, apathy and a lack of civic spirit result. The owner of the vacant land, very possibly inherited from parents, who suddenly becomes a multi-millionaire when the developers come through, may be happy with their good fortune. Some of the rest of us—particularly if we believe such good fortune may someday befall us—may even feel some happiness in the good luck of a fellow human being. But the poor child whose family rents a sub-standard home on a working-class salary knows that she will never benefit from such free goodies. She will correctly deduce that she lives in a tiered society, where some receive free wealth and others must work for every penny. If she has read the story of the Little Red Hen,[2] she will quickly deduce that her society does not put much stock in the Hen's timeless pronouncement, since it seems to give cake pieces, and often much the largest ones, to those who appear to be doing nothing to help make the cake. Such a system is *unjust,* and ultimately we all pay a price both in damaged *solidarity* and a lack of coherence in our values.

Consistent with these considerations, all natural resources, including land used for commercial and residential purposes, should be considered part of our *Commons.* No small number of Americans enjoy large windfalls when they sell homes which have appreciated in value well beyond the rate of inflation due to shortages in the housing supply or the increased desirability of the neighborhoods in which they live (location, location, location!). A good friend of mine purchased, for $150,000, a modest two-bedroom bungalow in an older neighborhood in the inner suburbs of Washington, D.C., in the late 1990s. This

2. Pg. 39

neighborhood, shortly after he purchased, became a "hot" one where wealthy buyers were tearing down the modest, 1940s structures and erecting elaborate McMansions. He sold the house a mere five years later for $450,000, walking away from the deal with $300,000 he had done nothing to earn. In the Wild West mentality which we have come to accept as normal, many will simply applaud his good luck (or perhaps his astute purchase). The provision of ten years worth of salary at $15 an hour, however, to an individual who has produced no goods or services in exchange, is an appalling instance of injustice, and an absolute refutation of the idea that we live in a merit-based society.

But surely, you are now saying, you don't mean to suggest that we cannot even own our own houses? And you would be correct, I am not proposing that we cannot own our houses. Our *houses*—that is, the structures we live in—are made objects, not natural resources, and in accordance with our concept of property, individuals should be able to exclusively own those things they create through their own efforts (or are created by others and then purchased from them). So, yes, we would own our houses. *But we would not own the land upon which they are built.* Instead, this land, like all natural resources, would be considered part of the *Commons*. It would be collectively owned, with the government as its steward, and leased for purposes in accord with local land-use plans. These leases would be of long term: in the case of private residences, for the duration of occupation of the dwelling by the lessee. When owners wish to sell their homes, buyers would take over the land-lease, paying the government for the use of the land. They would pay a purchase price to the current owner for any *structures* on the land, as well as improvements to those structures or the property itself. However, all unearned appreciation in value—the large majority of which typically consists of the land itself (location, location, location!)—would go back into the collective, not as a windfall to a private individual (and to the bank which will mortgage the property to the next hypothecated owner at a large profit in interest). Though this concept may seem outlandish to many modern readers, "ground rent," as this practice is called, was once very common in America.[3] Based on local master plans for development, America's future social democratic governments will lease not only residential but also commercial plots for designated purposes. Developers of commercial projects will become tenants of the land, with leases of long-enough term to recapture investments in built structures, the objective always being to keep within the *Commons* that which is truly common and, respecting the Little Red Hen, to eliminate the injustice of unearned windfalls from the appreciation of land values.

Current owners of land will not, of course, suffer uncompensated expropriation of their property. This would be both exceedingly unfair and inimical to one of the most basic premises of our constitution (the Fifth Amendment, prohibiting takings without "just compensation"). Instead, as real estate changes owners, the government will buy the land portion of the property at market value, charging a ground-rent going forward. These purchases will not upset public coffers, for they can be financed with bonds the interest of which will be paid with moneys derived from the ground rents.[4]

I understand that the idea of owning land in fee simple is deeply ingrained in the Anglo-American system of law and philosophy, as well as in our day-to-day experience, and would not expect this proposal to be an easy sell with the voting public. This is probably an idea for the 22nd, not the 21st Century. A more palatable way to achieve the basic purpose of eliminating unearned windfalls through land appreciation

---

3. Following a similar logic, the book *Progress and Poverty*, by American social philosopher Henry George, advocated deriving all taxes from real estate. The book sold over two million copies when it appeared in 1879.

4. To approximate our current system of fee simple ownership and the security it brings, especially to seniors, ground rents for a primary residence could be commuted after a stated period (for example, 30 years) for the original lease-holder(s).

would be to simply tax that portion of real estate sales constituting land value appreciation at something approximating 100 percent. However, for intellectual coherence, if we accept the premise that naturally occurring features should be the property of the Commons, and not private individuals, we will one day come around to putting all natural resources within common ownership.

One of the substantial advantages of placing natural resources within the *Commons* where they belong is the resulting reduction of the tax burden on average citizens. Governments—state, local or federal—will now be collecting ground rents and leasing payments for extractive resources on a universal scale, rather than these unearned funds going to private parties and banks (through their profits on mortgage loans). These inputs to government treasuries will go a long way toward funding necessary government operations without penalizing entrepreneurial and other truly productive activity.

The Built Environment and Protecting our Earth Home

Our conception of the *Commons* in our social democratic future will go beyond raw natural resources to include also the communal spaces in which we live. Having left behind the Lockean fetish of absolute rights for private property owners, we will undertake the task of creating communities that truly answer to human needs. Through intelligent planning we will create towns and cities that are safe and walkable: where the pedestrian is not in constant danger of being run down by automobiles; with built structures that are aesthetically pleasing; and with the abundant green spaces which *homo sapiens* requires for psychic well-being. We will abate harmful noise through the regulation of traffic and machinery, along with building codes that will require multi-family residences to be fitted with sound-proofing sufficient to allow tenants to hear themselves think and to sleep soundly at night. We will choose urban lighting schemes to eliminate light pollution, so that town and urban dwellers might enjoy a vital part of their birthright, the view of the stars at night.

If any of this sounds pie-in-the-sky it is only because we modern Americans have been told that we cannot have anything better than our chaotic, dangerous, noisy, inconvenient and inhuman common spaces. Renaissance Europe, with far fewer resources than we have today, created towns that today's global travelers crowd into to marvel at the beauty of the built structures and at the restful, pleasing and inspirational effect of the entirety of the built community on the human psyche. Several cities and towns in social democratic Great Britain, Spain, Portugal and Germany are in our 21st Century creating pedestrian-only center cities and towns, and *it is working*. To those who argue that we cannot afford such a vision—one of a life fit for human beings—I would say that our current system chiefly benefits those whose sole goal is to make the maximum possible profit from the development of built spaces, while providing as little value as possible to those who must live in them. It is not that we do not have the resources to engineer living spaces more suitable to *homo sapiens*; it is that those who build these spaces, and the politicians who represent their interests, have convinced the rest of us that nothing more is possible. Meanwhile they, with the exorbitant profits they make, move to quiet communities full of green spaces and aesthetically pleasing structures, where *they* can sleep soundly and see the stars at night.

Finally, as the custodian of the Commons, it goes almost without saying that governments in America's social democratic future will do whatever is required to keep our air, water and soil clean and pure, maintain wild spaces, protect biodiversity and stabilize the earth's climate.

Nuts & Bolts: Social Insurance

My discussion of social insurance, a key component of any social democratic system, will be brief. A couple of the key pillars of social support systems in social democracies—unemployment insurance and income support—will be covered by the system of living wages for guaranteed employment or training described earlier. Under that system every able-bodied and able-minded citizen will be guaranteed employment at a living wage, or if this is not available, upskilling at that same living wage. Those who are able-bodied and able-minded and refuse to sincerely participate in work or training, as already noted, will be on their own as regards income. The differently-abled who cannot be accommodated in the workplace will receive whatever support is needed to allow them lives of security and dignity.

Affordable healthcare, including dental and vision, will be universal. The precise system used is not, in my opinion, critical, but merely that every U.S. citizen has access to healthcare which is affordable at their level of income. I will note here that even the unwilling (able-bodied and minded adults who simply refuse to make a contribution) will have access to the same healthcare as others.

Old-age pensions will continue along the lines already achieved through Social Security, with the minimum benefits set at the living-wage level. The retirement age for those in arduous or hazardous occupations, those suffering from an occupation-related illness, or those who began work at an early age will be earlier than for others. One addition to support for the elderly will be affordable long-term care insurance, to enable seniors to age in place where possible or otherwise maintain a maximum level of independence into old age. This is currently a major gap the U.S. safety net, as Medicare does not cover such programs and Medicaid coverage does not apply until individuals are in deep poverty.

Nuts & Bolts:

Funding America's Social Democratic Future

We social democrats, like 2017 French presidential candidate Benoit Hamon, *believe in the public function.*[1] Unlike many American conservatives, we do not take an antagonistic attitude toward government (Ronald Reagan, in his inaugural address: "Government is not the solution to our problem, *government is the problem"),* nor do we consider government to be a "necessary evil." To the contrary, convinced that *homo sapiens* is a deeply social species, we think it inevitable that we organize ourselves in common purpose, while also allowing plenty of free rein for that individualism which is the other vital aspect of our complicated human nature.

Feeling, as we do, that government is not merely necessary and good, but an inescapable expression of the social nature of our species, we are not apologetic about using its powers for the general good. And since government action requires funding, we are not apologetic about applying taxes to income and wealth in order to support public programs. The only considerations in regard to government programs should be whether they are beneficial to the citizenry as a whole and whether they are operated efficiently. In regard to taxation itself, our key consideration will be whether distribution of the tax burden honors the social democratic values of *justice* and *solidarity.*

Funding a Social Democratic Future: Non-tax Sources of Revenue

Before considering taxation, properly speaking, let's look at two sources of non-tax revenue which will be available to government in our social democratic future.

One of these sources has already been alluded to in my discussion on the Commons (p. 76). When government rightly

------

1. p. 22 above

takes ownership of all natural resources, it will begin to collect substantial moneys in rents and leases. In such a system, profits earned solely through the ownership of those things rightly belonging to the collective of the nation's citizenry (the Commons) will flow to the national collective, rather than ending up in the accounts of private land owners, banks (in the form of loan interest) or resource-extraction enterprises. The U.S. Bureau of Economics reported, in 2009, the total rental value of all land in the U.S. at $1.15 trillion per year. According to the Tax Policy Center, total taxes paid to federal, state and local government in 2018 totaled $5.4 trillion. Using these admittedly extremely rough figures, which do not account for the significant value of leases for the exploitation of mineral, forest and agricultural lands, we can see that rent payments to government for use of the Commons would supply a significant portion of needed tax revenues.

Taking its rightful ownership of the Commons, then, will give government coffers a substantial boost. But government will still require other sources of revenue to make up the remainder of its budget. In considering where to find this revenue, one primary consideration will be the distinction between *earned* income and *unearned* income.

Social democrats believe in rewards based on merit, one area in which we are in complete agreement with most conservatives (or at least the claims made by most conservatives). We celebrate entrepreneurialism, the accumulation of professional skills and knowledge and the striving for excellence; and we honor those individuals who take on burdens greater than others or develop unique skills and talents to provide value to their fellow citizens. We don't mind if these high-value-producing individuals gain rewards greater than others (the fable of the Kingdom and the Bridge) though we still recognize government's right to regulate and tax any property assigned to them as it sees fit, and we will look askance if those rewards become exorbitant.

About rewards received, whether income or wealth, with

no corresponding value provided to society, we take a different view. When individuals receive windfalls through inheritance, or through the appreciation of land values, we see the principle of reward for merit perverted. We ask all citizens to participate in a social contract in which they are told that if they play by the rules and work hard they will receive rewards commensurate with the effort they have applied and the talents and skills they bring to the table. What then do we say, to those who are working hard to achieve the rewards on offer, when those who hire them to maintain their homes or repair their cars (or, for that matter, write up their legal documents) make no contribution at all to the collective effort, and in some cases never have and never will? The Little Red Hen would surely be displeased, seeing that we have allowed some who have not helped *make* the cake participate in *eating* the cake and—what's worse—often getting by far the largest slices.

Easily the most egregious form of unearned wealth is inheritance. A twenty-year-old heir or heiress of $100 million, without ever having spent one hour making any contribution to the collective welfare, will immediately enjoy control of a huge portion of the output of the American economy, output created by fellow citizens most of whom must labor from schooling until retirement. This individual will have others build their multiple homes, construct and pilot the jets on which they fly around the world amusing themselves and attend to their every need or even whim. There can certainly be no justification for this state of affairs: certainly no way to tell the cleaning person who scrubs the heir or heiress's floors that it is *just* that they must do backbreaking labor to make a living for the benefit of those who contribute nothing to our economic production. The injustice is perhaps less when the inheritance is $1 million rather than $100 million, or only $100,000 or $50,000. But the principle is the same. If we truly aspire and claim to be an economy based on merit, gaining economic rewards for free should have no place.

It might be argued, and I will agree, that the inherited wealth, *at some point*, was likely gained through merit. Some parent, grandparent, or great-great grandparent likely contributed significant value to society in order to accumulate enough wealth to leave substantial sums to heirs. And some will argue that if I have accumulated wealth through making a positive contribution to our common prosperity, I should be able to dispose of whatever wealth remains to me after paying taxes in whatever manner I choose. In general terms I would agree, with this caveat: your capacity to control the wealth you gain through productive effort ends when you die. After all, our philosophical justification for allowing some to gain greater rewards than others is that we thereby incentivize those who are willing and able to make greater-than-average contributions to society (the Kingdom and the Bridge). The enrichment of heirs does the opposite, however: those who inherit wealth have less or, if the inheritance is large enough, *no* material incentive to make any contribution to society. Meanwhile the spectacle of watching heirs and heiresses live in luxury through no efforts of their own, while others must work hard to earn their keep, makes a lie of the merit-based society, damages solidarity and discourages the working population, who cannot help but perceive that they are participating in a rigged game.

A defender of inheritance might make the more reasonable claim that, in allowing accumulated wealth to be passed on to heirs, we are indeed incentivizing ambitious individuals to make greater-than-average contributions to our prosperity. The idea here is that the capacity to pass on wealth to heirs, so that they will not need to work as hard as the ancestor who accumulated it, or so that, in some cases, they may live in luxury and ease, can be a motivator of productive economic effort. I would agree that there is probably some truth in this argument. There are no doubt those who, to some extent, find the idea of creating a legacy for their descendants, or a trouble-free life for their children, attractive. This possibility likely, I would also agree, adds *some* degree of incentive for *some* people. I would argue, however, that this is a perverse incentive, and while it may help spur some people, to some degree, to offer economic benefits to our collective benefit, the downsides (which include *disincentivizing* their heirs from making *any* productive effort) far outweigh any possible gain in productivity.

Inheritance's perversion of justice, the discouragement of workers and its damage to solidarity have already been mentioned. In addition to these downsides, serious enough in themselves, is yet another, and that is the tendency of inherited wealth to accumulate over generations and grow, leading to inter-generational aristocracies of wealth and privilege. Aside from the grotesque injustice of generations upon generations in a family line making no contribution to our collective efforts while having access to exorbitant proportions of the economic output the rest of us create, these wealthy families also end up in a position to exercise an outsized influence on politics (both the Koch Brothers and Donald Trump were heirs of substantial family fortunes). As has already been stated, rejection of hereditary aristocracy was a founding idea of this Republic, and in allowing unlimited inheritance we have allowed new aristocracies to be created.

In our social democratic future all, or nearly all, wealth accumulated during a person's lifetime will revert to the state when that person dies (a spouse will continue to enjoy possession of the couple's property until their death, of course). Otherwise we will permit only small bequests, to allow for the transmission of objects of sentimental value: on the order, perhaps, of $10,000 per heir in 2024 dollars. To prevent individuals from end-running these rules by making large gifts to others during their lifetimes, such transfers will either be strictly controlled or taxed so heavily as to make them unattractive.

Many will find the notion of ending inheritance deeply shocking. We have been conditioned to believe that descendants should be able to take over property owned by their ancestors upon those ancestors' deaths. But there is no law of human nature that dictates that this must be so. In ancient Athens, for instance, cropland was regularly re-distributed as families grew or declined in size. The more precise objection will be raised that ending inheritance (along with the placing of crop and grazing lands into the Commons) will end the storied "family farm" (though the vast majority of our foodstuffs are produced by huge corporate agribusinesses) as well as small "family businesses." While it might make sense for parents to instruct their minor children in the running of a farm or business, this does not change our analysis of whether or not these children have a right to the wealth their parents have earned in return for the contribution they've made to their fellow citizens. In a fair society, with rewards based upon merit, these children, like all others, must provide value themselves in order to achieve rewards. Having inside knowledge of the operation of their parents' farm or business, however, will place them in a prime position to purchase the business, at fair market value, upon the parents' death. If they have truly learned the lessons of their parents, they should have no trouble making a go of things. The question we must ask ourselves here is, "Do we want a society based on family dynasties of wealth and privilege, or one based upon rewards given for contributions made?"

The capturing of the wealth of deceased citizens will provide a boost more than twice the size of that provided by properly managing the Commons. According to a 2022 article on Bloomberg News, Americans are expected to inherit a total of $73 *trillion* dollars over the next twenty-five years. That comes to an annual average of $2.88 *trillion* dollars. The U.S. federal budget for 2021 called for roughly $6 trillion in spending. So, using these loose figures, if we take the value of inheritances per year ($2.88T) and add to that rents and leases on the Commons, properly considered ($1.15T, and this figure does not include leases for extractive activities on government land) we arrive at a figure which would cover approximately two-thirds of today's federal government budget. And this has been achieved solely by capturing unearned wealth (that produced by ownership of the Commons or through inheritance). Further revenues will be needed, of course, for both federal and state and local needs, and for these government will need to turn to taxation proper.

Government's Right to Tax: The Philosophical Justification

We saw, in our discussion of the Commons, that it is government alone which decides *who owns what* (through deeds and court systems), and that it is only by virtue of government-provided police protection that anyone can enjoy exclusive use of that property which government assigns to their possession. We might add here that, beyond the basic functions of recording deeds and maintaining a police force, government also creates money and controls its value, charters banks, enforces contracts, permits those hopelessly in debt to breach these contracts and start over through bankruptcy, and recognizes inheritance—thereby affecting everything from the fortunes of stock market investors and holders of debt to the price of goods, wage scales and the unemployment rate—and in myriad other ways determines the rules of the game through which property is acquired, held and exchanged. If it is the collective, then, which sets up and maintains a system regulating the acquisition, holding and exchange of property, the collective certainly has the right to determine how much of that property each citizen should relinquish back to the state to continue to *maintain that system.* Property *only* exists because of government. This would seem, to me, to give government an irrefutable claim in regards to its uses, including the use of taxation to support government functions. Differently put, if government is the ongoing determiner of *who owns what,* we might say that, at tax time, the government is merely making due and necessary adjustments to our various *who-owns-what* accounts.

If I labor here to convince you that government has a virtually unlimited right to tax wealth and income as it sees fit, it is because the idea that we, as individuals, have some claim over property which government cannot disturb is deeply embedded in our political discourse. If we speak of billionaires like Bill Gates or Jeff Bezos paying a wealth tax (as did Elizabeth Warren during her 2020 presidential campaign), many are those who say: "They earned it, and the government has no right to take it." What is not added, and perhaps not understood, is that they "earned it" thanks to the fact that the government maintains an economic system in which earning that money was possible (the maintenance of a currency, the enforcement of contracts, the protection of copyrights, etc.) and that they enjoy its possession only because the collective, acting through government (the police) is willing to protect it for them. (Never mind the further question as to whether it can truly be said that, when a wealthy person puts 100 million dollars into real estate investments and five years later the value of these properties has grown to 200 million dollars, that the wealthy person has, in any normal sense, "earned" the additional 100 million dollars.)

I will not attempt here to precisely specify how U.S. governments will achieve the tax revenues needed to support our social democratic future beyond what is gained through proper management of the Commons and the reversion of estates (this will require real-time deliberations by hosts of economists and politicians), but will instead establish some basic principles. One of these is perhaps obvious, and that is that tax revenue must come from where such revenue exists. This means that those living at a basic living wage will continue to pay little in taxes, as is the case today. It also means that those with progressively more income and wealth will pay progressively more in taxes. Modern conservatives sing the loud and constant refrain that raising tax rates on the wealthy (e.g., the Biden administration proposal to raise taxes on incomes over $450,000) will stifle entrepreneurialism and eventually lead to general poverty. This claim is absurd to anyone familiar with mid-twentieth-century America, for top tax rates during the 1950s and 1960s, the most dynamic economic era of modern American history (with average annual growth above 4%, as opposed to something less than 2% in the first two decades of this century), were multiples of what they are today.

Another canard that conservative interests often repeat is the mantra that if taxes are raised on business owners they will stop or slow hiring, thereby hurting wage and salaried workers. Either those making these claims do not understand how business owners think, or they are intentionally misstating reality (I have owned and operated a business for several decades myself, so I have some personal insight into this matter.) For any business owner with a workable business model, each employee is a *profit center*. My business is not a charity, and if I hire a new worker it is for one reason only: because I believe that they will produce more revenue for the company than what they are paid in salary and benefits, thereby resulting in an increase in my, the business owner's, income. If I were to learn that the government had decided to take a greater share of my profits from the business in taxes, my incentive would be to try all the harder to *add* employees, thereby raising my pre-tax revenue in order to maintain my after-tax income at the accustomed level. The last thing I would do would be to terminate employees, each one a source of revenue, thereby *decreasing* my income.

In keeping with our commitment to favoring merit-based income over rentier income, we will tax income made by owning non-productive assets (precious metals, works of art, etc.) at higher rates than income gained through work. We will re-examine *copyrights* and patents and make sure that the length of these rights does not go further than the minimum necessary to incentive creativity and innovation. We will not look askance at income earned through stocks and bonds, as the purchase of shares or debt of an ongoing business (or government) represents forgoing the present enjoyment of one's income to the benefit of a productive enterprise: it should be taxed like any other income. We will not be shy about taxing wealth, both because this is where a great deal of disposable assets can be found and also because we do not believe that large fortunes are justifiable or healthy for a functioning social democracy built on the values of justice, solidarity and radical inclusion. As a very rough figure, I will state that there is probably very little to be gained, from the point of view of incentivizing productive effort, and much to lose, by allowing anyone to control more than $100,000,000 in assets. Valued added taxes (or sales taxes) should be applied to goods at the wholesale level, with special focus on luxury items. This will skew the VAT tax burden away from daily necessities of those living at the basic living wage and will have the added benefit of discouraging conspicuous consumption, which is damaging to solidarity and inclusion and ruinous for the planet.

An argument frequently made against taxing the wealthy— often innovators and prime movers in the production of valuable goods and services—is that such individuals will expatriate themselves and/or their wealth and income, leaving the rest of us all the poorer. First, I consider it unlikely that many entrepreneurs would wish to operate anywhere other than the world's largest economy, nor give up the great good fortune of citizenship in the world's most powerful and influential nation. It is already current law that income earned anywhere in the world by a U.S. citizen is taxable by the U.S. government. The principle could also be established that wealth earned in the United States is taxable by the U.S. government regardless of where the earner decides to live or to park that wealth; wealth being expatriated could also be subject to "exit taxes" at such a rate as to make moving one's capital out of the United States a very unattractive proposition. We social democrats value entrepreneurs for what they bring to American society, but it is American society—with its many intelligent laws, civic institutions, stable currency and government-educated citizenry—that creates the basis for business success.

Nuts & Bolts:

Democracy in America's Social Democratic Future

To state the obvious, with apologies, a critical aspect of social democracy is . . . *democracy*. We social democrats believe that, to the extent possible, the citizens of a nation should have the final say in how they are governed, and also that every citizen should, to the extent possible, have an *equal* say in how they are governed. We Americans are fortunate to live in a nation where, in the main, democratic practices are long established and still functioning. From the first founding of the Republic, when the franchise was limited through property qualifications to a small fraction of the adult male population; through the granting of universal white male suffrage; the official granting of the franchise to newly freed enslaved people after the Civil War (often denied, admittedly, on a de facto basis); the direct election of senators (who, for the first one hundred years of the nation, were selected by state legislators); the extension of the vote to women in 1920; and on to a fuller commitment to minority voting rights with the Voting Rights Act of 1967, the U.S. has steadily, if slowly, come ever closer to that nation "of the people, by the people and for the people" invoked by Lincoln at Gettysburg. But though it might reasonably be said that we have largely achieved one of the two ideals stated at the head of this paragraph—that the citizenry have final say—we still have a substantial road to walk to achieve the second of those ideals: that all citizens have an *equal* say.

To begin with, the very organization of the federal government of the United States does not provide each citizen with equal influence. The two great offenders here are the U.S. Senate and the Electoral College. Taking the Senate, the 10 least populated states, with roughly three percent of the total U.S. population, control 20 percent of U.S. Senate seats. Each citizen of these smaller states therefore has between six and seven times more voting power in the U.S. Senate than the average American. The citizens of California, who make up nearly 12 percent of the total U.S. population, only control two percent of the U.S. Senate—which gives each California resident 1/6th the voting power of the average American in the U.S. Senate, and only 1/68th the voting power of residents of Wyoming, the least populous state. Viewed from another angle, states representing just 17 percent of the U.S. population could theoretically command a 51 percent majority in the Senate, allowing them to lord it over the remaining 83 percent of the U.S. population. As it happens, in today's Senate (2023), there are 50 Republicans and 50 Democrats, although the Democrat senators represent 40 million more American voters than the Republican. This is *not* majority rule, nor is it equal representation for all. It affords a minority of the population an ongoing veto against the will of the majority of citizens.

The simplest remedy to this egregious violation of democratic principles would be to abolish the Senate altogether. Many modern nations—among them advanced social democracies such as Denmark, Finland, Iceland, New Zealand, Norway and Sweden—function perfectly adequately with a unicameral legislature. A less radical change would be to keep the Senate but either (1) calibrate the number of senators in each state to that state's population, or (2) keep two senators per state but weight senators' votes in proportion to their states' populations.

Much like the current Senate, the Electoral College gives smaller states a disproportionate impact in presidential elections. It should be abolished.

The gerrymandering practiced by state legislators in both

major parties is another stain on American democracy. Majority parties creatively draw congressional district boundaries specifically in order to dilute the voting strength of voters who favor the opposition. Legislative districts should be drawn by independent bodies, based solely on objective, scientific criteria with the single goal of achieving equal power for each vote cast. Rank-choice voting is another step that would help assure that the votes of those supporting parties not in the majority not be wasted and their voices heard.

Another major impediment to a fuller expression of the democratic ideal in the United States today is the role of money in politics. Political campaigns, especially those for major offices, have become tremendously expensive. In the age of mass communications, voters are reached more through mass mailings, radio and television spots than through in-person gladhanding, and these things are not cheap. In the 2020 federal election cycle nearly $4 billion was spent directly by congressional candidates, with political parties spending an additional $3.2 billion and political action committees spending a whopping $12.9 billion. While outspending an opponent does not guarantee victory (in the 2020 battle for the Democratic presidential nomination, Bernie Sanders spent about $46 million as against Biden's roughly $13 million, and we know the result),[1] it is nonetheless true that it requires money, and very large sums of it, to run for major political offices. Even state legislature candidates are now spending $1 million or more on campaigns. And while money can be raised in many ways, including by pooling small donations, it goes without saying that those with access to donors with large amounts of cash, or candidates who are themselves wealthy, have a major advantage in raising the funds needed to mount a political campaign in modern times. There is no way that each citizen can have an equal say in choosing our leaders or, for that matter, running for office, when a billionaire can fund her campaign without soliciting a single donation, and a well-connected Wall Street operator has access to a large

1. Reuters, March 21, 2020

body of wealthy friends and associates, while the average citizen does not. It is further inevitable that those candidates who propose laws favorable to entrenched moneyed interests will find it far easier to fund their campaigns than those who seek a fairer distribution of the nation's economic output. These same entrenched moneyed interests are also in a position to mount campaigns in support of candidates who cater to their interests through massive, largely unregulated expenditures of *dark money*.

While I agree that modern forms of mass communications (film and television, radio broadcasts, books and print journalism) are forms of expression protected by the First Amendment of the U.S. Constitution, the Supreme Court has also ruled, throughout generations, that this First Amendment right, like other constitutional rights, is not illimitable. Famously, one cannot shout "Fire!" in a crowded theater, nor defame others, nor incite others to sedition and insurrection. Where a countervailing interest is greater than the value of one's capacity to express oneself, the right of free expression *can* be limited by government.

I would hold that there is no greater interest in our democratic republic than ensuring that every adult citizen has an equal say in how we are governed and an equal right to participate in the political process through running for, and holding, elective office. The fact is that money, and the unequal access to money among our citizenry, perverts our democratic principles, making some far more equal than others when it comes to political influence. This unequal distribution of money in society gives those with outsized resources a greater capacity to fund the candidates and issues that serve their interests. It allows them to essentially "own" candidates who do their bidding once in office, for these candidates, looking to the next election cycle, must be careful to keep their donors happy. Those with great amounts of discretionary wealth are also in a position, especially since the notorious *Citizens United* case, to expend unlimited sums to influence public opinion.

The simple, common-sense solution to this predicament is the public funding of political campaigns. After reaching an established threshold of signatures on a petition, or after achieving a fund-raising threshold in donations limited to an amount any citizen could be expected to afford (say, $25), a candidate will be eligible for a fixed amount of public funding to hire staff, create and send mailings, and to purchase TV and radio time. If we wished to economize on these expenditures, much of the TV and radio exposure could potentially come through PBS and NPR stations, in periodic candidate forums in which each candidate would be given an equal amount of time to share their proposals with voters. Weekly broadsheets could be published and mailed at government expense, or distributed online, with each qualified candidate again given an equal amount of space.

The other important leg of this system is that, after qualifying, candidates will not be allowed to spend any moneys beyond these publicly provided resources, including their own funds. The goal of the system will be to create as completely a level playing field as possible, with each candidate having equal resources to reach voters with their message.

Issue advocacy would be permitted by private groups and individuals, but limits would be placed on their funding sources, with donation caps set at levels that would ensure that moneyed interests do not unfairly dominate the public debate.

Nut & Bolts:

Crime and ~~Punishment~~ Rehabilitation

Crime, and particularly violent crime, is a policy area where the American Left is typically—and often successfully—"owned" by the American Right. A recent Gallup poll found that only 27% of Americans are satisfied with "the nation's policies to reduce or control crime." A 2022 Pew Research poll found that 61% of Americans (and 81% of Americans racialized as "Black") say that violent crime is a "very important" driver of their voting decisions; and a 2016 poll by Morning Star/Vox found that only 29% think sentences for violent crimes should be reduced.[1]

For the average voter, the Democratic Party is seen as being "soft" on crime, reluctant to impose what many see as sufficiently stern measures to deter bad actors from breaking rules the rest of us consent to live by: ranging from heinous acts of violence to less destructive acts such as theft and even illegal border crossings. Conservative politicians call for longer sentences than their Democratic counterparts who, self-identifying as the kinder, gentler political alternative (and beholden to identity constituencies whose self-proclaimed spokespersons frequently oppose crime remediation measures that disproportionately impact those they claim to speak for) typically remain silent on the issue, perhaps hoping that it will "just go away."

The American Left's (as embodied by the Democratic Party) silence on the issue of crime, and especially violent crime,

_____

1. https://www.pewresearch.org/short-reads/2022/10/31/violent-crime-is-a-key-midterm-voting-issue-but-what-does-the-data-say/; https://www.vox.com/2016/9/7/12814504/mass-incarceration-poll

has and will continue to cost the party dearly, both in electoral defeats and intellectual incoherence. Let me state a couple fundamental principles before moving on to a detailed examination of how the American Left got itself into this position, and then some proposals for the future. The first principle is this: Every citizen of this nation, or any nation, no matter where they live, should be entitled to go about their lawful business, to walk the streets and abide in their homes and workplaces, without having to fear becoming victims of violent assault. Social democrats like myself strongly believe in protecting the safety and well-being of each and every citizen, from the poorest child to the most powerful leader. This is why we support such measures as universal healthcare, unemployment insurance, workplace safety rules, clean air and water and adequate old-age pensions. How can we then not be outraged when one of our fellow citizens is set upon and violently attacked resulting, if not in death, then in lifelong impairment: physical, psychological or both? Looked at from another angle, we can assert that it is a fundamental duty of any state which claims to operate for the benefit of its citizens to protect their physical safety, whether this be from poverty, lack of healthcare, invasion by foreign powers, air and water pollution, unsafe food, harmful medications . . . or violent attack by a fellow citizen.

Though non-violent offenses create less harm, we can also state the principle that any citizen should be secure in their possessions. In the social democratic polity we aim to create, where material rewards are based on merit (and remembering Hume's assertion that the key purpose of the state is to determine *who owns what*), the state must see that citizens are not disturbed in the possession of the material things which their hard work and dedication to serving their fellow-citizens have earned them. We social democrats also very strongly believe in another foundational principle: the *rule of law*. We believe that in a nation operating under the premises of democracy citizens, in exchange for having a say in how they are governed and by whom, agree to follow the rules established by the governments they have chosen. We social democrats believe that the law must be applied to all equally, regardless of social or economic status, for we understand that the alternatives are either anarchy and chaos, or a tyrannical state where the law is applied in an *ad hoc* fashion depending on the self-interests of dictators. For this system to work, each citizen *must follow established laws.*

Criminal acts not only harm their victims, most severely in the case of violent crimes, but also weaken our entire society, causing all of us to live in fear, to avoid entire swaths of major cities and to invest incredible amounts of time, effort and money in protecting our possessions from theft. Crime, or rather its toleration by a complacent society, costs every one of us every day and diminishes our quality of life.

Having established these basic principles, let's consider how the American Left has gotten itself behind the eight ball in regard to crime. First let's note an interesting irony. Though the American Left generally looks more favorably upon government action (we don't agree with Ronald Reagan that "government is the problem"), there is also an undercurrent of anti-establishmentism going back to an "Old Left" which saw itself as representing the proletariat masses as against the "powers that be," a strain further nurtured in more recent times by the hippy movement of the 1960s. Thus we find Seattle mayor Jenny Durkin stating in a CNN interview that the violent occupation, during the pandemic, of a six-block area of downtown Seattle by anarchist hooligans would perhaps just become another "Summer of Love." (Durkin, after being called on the statement, claimed that she "clearly [to her, perhaps] said that in jest" but admitted that "it probably was not the smart thing to do"). One might wonder at a major city mayor "jesting" about a violent insurgency which took over part of her city, excluding law enforcement from the area, destroying property and providing the context to a fatal shooting, but in any case the damage was done; the

Right made hay, and rightly so, with Durkin's ill-conceived remarks. Durkin had burnished her "hipster" credentials and ingratiated herself with radical youth and the "Occupy Wall Street" movement, but she had done considerable damage to the Democratic Party's image in the eyes of the vast majority of Americans. Her statement, coupled with her refusal to take adequate measures to end the illegal takeover of the city center, made a mockery of the social democratic foundational principle of the *rule of law.*

Most Americans follow every law (with the probable exception, for some, of speed limits) and are unhappy when others are allowed to break them with impunity. (This is not merely out of envy, I would posit, but stems from the conviction that our laws are not merely justified, having been formulated by democratically elected governments, but also that they are in the main good: that is, reflective of the consensus among most people about the rules we should live by.) The American Left cannot have it both ways. We cannot both tout the rule of law *and also* be complacent about law-breaking. The inescapable corollary of a democratic polity based on the rule of law, which requires the application of laws impartially and indiscriminately, is that citizens *must follow the laws that are made.*

Another complication in the American Left's approach to crime is the Democratic Party's proud and historic (at least since the Sixties) role as champion of racially-defined minorities that have been subjected to unequal treatment, particularly Americans racialized as "Black" (ARBs). There is a long history of ARBs being denied all due process, summarily judged and lynched, or bullied, battered and killed by police with impunity. It is also a well-known fact that ARBs make up a significantly disproportionate share of the American prison population (this last is chiefly explained, it should be said, by the fact that Americans racialized as "Black," as a statistically defined group, commit crimes at rates considerably greater than those of Americans racialized as "White.")[2] In all events,

2. https://en.wikipedia.org/wiki/Race_and_crime_in_the_United_

the "war on drugs" has been particularly damaging in communities where ARBs are predominant, criminalizing many for the mere possession of psychotropic substances. All of these factors have contributed to a merging of two otherwise disparate issues: crime and racial discrimination. That is, it has become difficult to discuss crime in America without the issue of past and present discrimination against ARBs strongly coloring, if not controlling, the dialogue. A common cry, when stiffer criminal penalties have been proposed, has often been, "We can't put any more young Black men in jail!" It is even argued, indirectly if not directly, that criminal behavior by ARBs is somehow excusable, or might be overlooked, given the discrimination to which their racialized identity group has been subjected historically and (by some readings) into the present.[3] Most recently, concerns over "equity," based upon the theory that all disparate outcomes are, ipso facto, caused by systemic racism, have led several big-city DAs to forego the prosecution of entire categories of criminal behavior where the application of the law would result in a disproportionate impact on ARBs.

This is, in my view, all very unfortunate, because it leads on the conceptual level to intellectual incoherence, and on the practical level to a stalemated situation where nothing can be

States; https://ucr.fbi.gov/crime-in-the-u.s/2019/crime-in-the-u.s.-2019/tables/table-43

3. Many on the Left relativized the widespread looting, arson and violence against police and others committed by ARBs after the murder of George Floyd by Derek Chauvin, and also after the killing of Michael Brown by Ferguson, MO, police officer Darren Wilson; some called for completely dismantling police forces.. Ta-Nehisi Coates, whom *Washington Post* book critic Carlos Lozada has referred to as the thinker "to whom so many of us turn to affirm, challenge or more often mold our views," rails against the disproportionate incarceration of ARBs, chalking it up to a virtually intentional choice of an uncaring and systemically racist American society, rather than an unfortunate result of the simple fact that a far larger proportion of ARBs commit serious crimes than ARWs ("The Black Family in the Age of Mass Incarceration" in *The Atlantic*, October 2015)

done about the grave problem of violent crime—a problem that, as we have noted, is an affront to our social democratic values. Unless we propose to apply one set of crime remediation measures to Americans racialized as "White," and a different set to Americans racialized as "Black," then if we excuse criminal activity on the part of ARBs we must excuse the criminal activity of all. The cries from self-proclaimed spokespeople for ARBs were loud and vociferous (and rightly so) that Derek Chauvin be put in prison for a very long time (if not executed) for the murder of George Floyd. No one suggested looking into whether he had experienced a difficult or deprived childhood, or whether his parents failed to provide the love he needed or inculcated in him a proper respect for the safety and well-being of others.

We will do ourselves a great service if we can disconnect the discussion about crime from the discussion about race. First, it should be remembered that in America, people racialized as "White" commit the majority of all crimes and are the largest prison population. Even if it made sense (which I do not believe it does) to justify or overlook crimes committed by Americans racialized as "Black" in light of the ill-treatment to which their racialized group has historically been (and many would argue, continues to be) subjected, it is nonsensical in the extreme to allow ourselves to be terrorized by people of chiefly European ancestry. Further, it must be stated that the chief victims of violent criminals racialized as "Black" are other ARBs! If we claim to be helping ARBs by allowing them to commit crimes, we must admit that we are simultaneously *hurting* those ARBs who are the chief victims of those crimes. And if we refuse to segregate from the general population violent people with no respect for the rights or safety of others, on the theory that not they but the deprived or abusive environments in which they were raised are responsible for their crimes, we will have little justification for segregating any dangerous person from the general population. For I believe it can be safely stated, as a general rule, that a person who decides to make his way through the world by robbing, killing or raping was not raised in the most enlightened or nurturing fashion. In fact, if you look at the family backgrounds of the prison population of all ethnically or racially defined backgrounds you will find a sad story of childhood deprivation, neglect and abuse.

It might be helpful at this point to clarify that what I propose for our social democratic future, in regard to crime, is a system based not on the idea of "punishment" but founded instead upon concepts of public safety, the right of citizens to enjoy their lawfully acquired property, and *rehabilitation.* Let me further state that we will create a clear division in our thinking in regard to violent crimes against persons and other crimes.

Speaking first to violent crime, there is a longstanding concept within our culture that when a person commits a violent crime against another person, "justice" is served when the wrongdoer is visited with a "punishment" commensurate with the harm done to victims and those who love them. To me, this entire notion is starkly absurd; for I do not believe any of us can really know what "justice" would require in cases of criminal violence. On the one hand, how can you draw an equivalence between, say, brain damage inflicted by a violent attack with a baseball bat and 20 years in prison? Aren't we comparing apples and oranges? Will the 20-year prison term somehow make the person's brain better? If we were really committed to "an eye for an eye and a tooth for a tooth," the most appropriate "punishment" in such a case would be to inflict, through a baseball-bat beating, the same level of brain damage on the perpetrator as was inflicted on the victim. On the other hand, if a person is severely deprived, neglected or abused as a child, so that they are unable to control their impulses, or having been unloved do not know how to feel compassion toward others, is it really "just" to make them suffer further by depriving them of their freedom and social contacts? An injustice of sorts was already committed when the violent offender drew the short straw and ended up with parent(s) unable to provide an upbringing conducive to psychological and social adjustment. Justice on this cosmic scale is beyond our capacities; that is, I believe it is ridiculous to believe that we human beings, severely limited in our understanding, can apply "punishments" in such a way as to achieve moral "justice."

Given my earlier remarks, it should however be clear that I will not propose, just because we cannot discern absolute "justice," that we allow criminals to wreak havoc upon our communities. The difference in the approach I will propose is that our justification for removing the violent wrongdoer from the community is not to achieve moral "justice" by "punishing" the wrongdoer, but to ensure public safety by removing a patently dangerous individual from the general population and placing them somewhere where they can do no further harm. A further difference is that the extent to which we keep a violent lawbreaker segregated from others will not be determined by some notion of having, by inflicting an appropriate amount of "punishment," achieved "justice" (an eye for an eye, etc.) but will be determined by the public safety question of, "Is it safe to return this person to the general population?"

Incarceration serves two purposes. One, just outlined, is to protect the community by removing demonstrably dangerous individuals from the general population, keeping them apart so that they may do no further harm. The second purpose served by incarceration is deterrence: the fear of incarceration, a highly unpleasant experience, will make the prospective criminal think twice before committing a violent act, at least in those cases where the person involved is capable of exercising even the most elementary degree of rational, cost-benefit analysis.

The first of these premises is irrefutable: a person who has shown a capacity to commit violent acts cannot commit further such acts, at least not against the general public, while confined in a correctional facility. As to the second premise, the deterrent effect of incarceration, there is some debate. There are those, chiefly in the "don't lock up any more people" crowd, who loudly proclaim that "punishing" violent criminals with stiff prison sentences is useless, because "studies" show that fear of punishment does not deter the criminally minded. I can only repeat Mark Twain's remark here that there are lies, damnable lies, and statistics (i.e., "studies"). The idea that no one will be deterred from committing violent acts by the possibility of being put in prison is so ridiculous that no sane person should have to debate the question. It flies in the face of what each of us feels and knows to be true both of ourselves and our fellow human beings. The *actual* conclusion of the typically cited studies is that *increasing* penalties for specific crimes (beyond a previous baseline) has not been shown to serve as an *additional* deterrent, the reason being that *criminals are not generally aware of the precise sentences for specific crimes* in the first place, and therefore cannot be expected to change behavior when these sentences are increased (also without their awareness). So rather than argue that stiff prison sentences do not deter violent crimes (an absurd assertion which no study has proven), one would better argue that we need to make sure that prospective violent criminals are *very* aware of the consequences of committing violent acts. In our current system, with violent acts broken into a bewildering array of minutely defined categories, judges given a great deal of leeway in sentencing, and with the possibility of plea bargains always in the mix, it is not merely the prospective criminal who is unaware of the consequences of committing a violent act: the fact is that no one can know what the consequences of a specific violent crime will be, from legislator to judge, from attorney to the general citizenry. It is not surprising therefore that someone contemplating violent behavior may entertain the idea that they will get off with a "light" sentence, or "plead down." This is why, in the system I will propose, there will be no doubt whatsoever about the consequences of committing a serious violent crime.

Recidivism rates are over 60 percent for violent offenses and almost 80 percent for property offenses. This reflects the reality that a very large majority of both violent and property crimes are being committed by a cadre of repeat offenders who make a regular practice of criminal activity ("career criminals"). Regardless of whether the threat of long prison sentences would deter these individuals from continuing to engage in criminal activity (which I have no doubt it would, were the consequences invariable and well-publicized), one thing is beyond dispute: if these repeat offenders are in correctional institutions, they will not be committing these repeat crimes. In this sense, long prison sentences are unquestionably a deterrent in that they prevent repeat offenders (who are committing the majority of crimes) from offending further.

Those who advocate for keeping criminals out of jail argue from a place that incarceration is a tragedy visited upon the unfortunate armed robber, rapist or murderer. I would argue otherwise; and to explain my position, I must first share a couple of my general premises about human life. The first is my conception that the only thing that can really make life valuable is to be of benefit to one's fellow human beings. I also believe that we are innately moral beings, and I do not believe a life worthy of that name is possible without abiding by ancient moral laws that have formed the foundations of every world religion and higher philosophy in human memory. The Christian "golden rule," of which some version is found in every major religion, states a basic principle of this universal moral code very well: "do unto others as you would have them do unto you." The Buddhists say we should "do good, and if we cannot do good, at least do no harm." In my view, to allow a person to continue to rob, rape and murder does them no favors. It is in fact my view that anything one might do to prevent such an individual from further damaging their own moral life with indecent behavior, including incarceration, performs a capital service to that person. I can state unequivocally that if someone with a functional crystal ball were to tell me that two weeks from now I would commit an armed robbery, one year later a rape, and two years after that a murder, but that all of this could be prevented if I were immediately put in prison and kept there until I could learn to control my violent impulses, I would *beg* to be incarcerated. Better that than the stain on my psyche and, if I may use the phrase, immortal soul, should I be allowed to commit the heinously cruel acts foretold by the seer. No, we do not harm deranged, violent and self-obsessed people when we incarcerate them, thereby ensuring that they do not commit further harm against their fellow human beings. We provide them an invaluable service.

So, what will criminal response and remediation look like in our social democratic future? As already stated, it will be founded upon ideas of public safety, the right of citizens to enjoy their rightfully acquired property, and it will aim to rehabilitate. We will begin with a consideration of the violent offender, about whom we will apply special measures, as the harm they do is qualitatively different than that done by property crimes.

The first distinction we will make in our response to violent crime is that between (1) serious violent crimes and (2) lesser violent offenses. A "serious violent crime" will be defined as "any act that a reasonable person would know could conceivably cause life-impairing injuries (including disfigurement) or death to the victim." This category will also include rapes and all sexual crimes against minors. Within the category of "serious violent crimes" there will be three sub-categories: (1) serious violent crimes resulting in the death of the victim (2) serious violent crimes resulting in life-impairing injuries (including disfigurement) to the victim, as well as all rapes and child sexual abuse, and (3) serious violent crimes which did not, but could have, resulted in life-impairing injuries (including disfigurement) to the victim. Serious violent crime will include acts ranging from shooting someone with a gun to banging their head repeatedly against a brick wall.

Gone will be the current complicated system of dozens of violent crime definitions, with multiple gradations within each (first, second and third degree murder, various degrees of manslaughter, assault, and etc.). These distinctions are based upon the notion, which I reject, that the criminal response system should attempt to match a "punishment" to the moral severity of the crime, thereby arriving at "justice."

The system I propose here, first, will treat all "serious violent crimes," as defined in the last paragraph, which result in life-impairing injuries (including disfigurement), as well as rapes and child sexual abuse, the same. An individual found guilty of committing any such act, for a first offense, will be sentenced to 10 years to life in a correctional facility. An individual convicted of a serious violent crime which does not result in life-impairing injuries (including disfigurement), but which a reasonable person would know could have resulted in such injuries, will be sentenced to 5 years to life in a correctional facility.[4] Critically important to the moral coherence of this system, our correctional facilities will be fully oriented toward rehabilitation, and in a far more comprehensive manner than they are today. The goal of incarceration will not be to "punish" the wrongdoer (though we will benefit from the deterrent effect of the threat of imprisonment) but to attempt to alter their psyche in such a way as to render them no longer a threat to public safety. Taking it as a given that a person who can commit a serious violent act against a fellow citizen is in some manner psychologically ill, or at the very least not

4. It could be argued that a person who commits an act of violence that a reasonable person would know could cause life-impairing injuries, even if such injuries do not occur, is as great a public-safety concern as a person who commits a similar act which *does* result in life-impairing injuries. It can equally be argued, however, that the lack of actual life-impairing injuries may suggest a lesser attempt at harm on the part of the attacker, and thereby a lesser public-safety concern. In this case it might be said that the attacker "pulled their punches." Further, such a sentencing structure, in terms of deterrence, will give an attacker an incentive to *not* cause life-imparing injuries.

properly socialized, we will spare no effort or expense to help the perpetrator learn how to live among others. Correctional facilities will be abundantly staffed with mental health professionals, and inmates will benefit from continual treatment by therapists and psychiatrists. Inmates will also participate in systems of education, job training, work and communal living in order to reorient them toward living with others in a socially acceptable fashion. Access to media will be tightly supervised to prevent exposing inmates to nonconstructive influences. As noted, the sole sentence for all first offenses involving acts of serious violence resulting in life-impairing injuries (including disfiurement), as well as rape and child sexual abuse, will be 10 years to life (or 5 years to life for acts of serious violence which did not, but could have, resulted in life-impariing injuries or death). That is, 10 or 5 years will be the *minimum* amount of time an individual convicted of a serious violent crime will serve in a correctional facility. I claim no scientific basis for these time periods, but my intuition and life experience both tell me that 10 years, for acts resulting in life-impairing injuries as well as rape and child sexual abuse, or 5 years for acts did not, but could have resulted in life-impairing injuries, is roughly how long it would take both to turn someone's thinking around, and also to reassure the public that an adequate attempt has been made at rehabilitation. Education, job training, work and other communal activities as well as psychiatric treatment, as needed, will be mandatory, and refusal to participate in these programs will result in demerits. Demerits will also be earned by the commission of criminal acts against prison staff or other inmates or by failure to follow any established protocols. If the incarcerated individual participates in all required programs, avoids demerits, and receives the approval of a board consisting of prison management, mental-health staff, other supervisors and elected members of the community, they will be released after 10 (or 5) years. If instead they refuse to participate in rehabilitative programs, make insufficient progress, or commit further offenses, their time served will be extended further which, in the cases of the most recalcitrant, could result in life in prison.[5]

Acts of serious violence (as defined here) which result in death of the victim will require special treatment. From the point of view of public safety (that is, the danger the perpetrator poses to the public), there is little conceptual difference between hitting someone repeatedly and forcefully over the head with a baseball bat in a mindless rage, and they surviving the attack with a cracked skull, and shooting someone in the head with a firearm and killing them. In both cases the attacks could have resulted in death, and both provide irrefutable evidence that the perpetrator of such acts is a grave threat to his fellow citizens.[6] From a practical point of view, however, if there is no greater penalty for killing than for assaulting, there will be an incentive for perpetrators of violent attacks, including rapes, to kill their victims in order to eliminate what will often be the sole witness to the crime. For this reason, and also because the death of the victim may in some cases indicate an attempt to kill rather than merely injure (and thereby a greater threat to public safety), the sole sentence for serious violent crimes that result in the victim's death will be 20 years to life. Otherwise these perpetrators will undergo the same program as other serious violent offenders.

There are two major premises behind this proposed system. One is that public safety is paramount. Once an individual has demonstrated that they have not internalized the most important rule of our society—do not violently assail others—we have a duty to all peaceful citizens to isolate this person from the general population, restricting their movements until we can be *reasonably* sure that they are no longer a threat to public safety. The second premise here is that everyone deserves a second chance. Given the neglect, abuse and deprivation many are subjected to as children, it would seem only fair to make one major effort to aid violent offenders

6. See footnote on page 119: a similar logic applies here.

to mend their ways before writing them off. Hence a 5-to-10-year, heavily funded program of rehabilitation (or 20 in cases resulting in death of the victim).

Those who successfully complete a rehabilitative program of at least 5, 10 or 20 years (or longer, with demerits) will be free to circulate again in society. Copious assistance will be given at re-entry, in finding housing and getting connected with the employment and training Hub outlined in Chapter 1. If there is a second serious violent offense after release, however, the offender will be sent to a different type of facility: and here they will remain for life. Here the offender will be kept as comfortable as possible, but we will no longer focus on rehabilitation for re-entry into society. Our conception is that everyone is entitled to a second chance: one. It is reasonable to conclude that, if after completing the program once, apparently successfully, the violent offender commits a second act of serious violence, either such a person is impervious to our rehabilitation system or we do not have the means to determine when they are again safe to circulate freely. Thus, our system for serious violent offenders could be called a "two-strikes-and-you're-out" system.

This proposal possesses several major advantages over our current failed system. (1) From a point of view of public safety, it removes people who have demonstrated a propensity for serious violence from circulation until we can, with some reasonable certainty, conclude that they have learned to control their violent impulses. (2) This system will capture mainly repeat offenders (since most crime, and especially serious crime, is committed by repeat offenders), thereby removing the chief cause of criminal activity from our streets. (3) With so many fewer career criminals on the loose, police departments and our court systems can focus more efforts on apprehending those criminal offenders who are still at large (in some U.S. jurisdictions, the conviction rate for murder is less than 50%). (4) Instead of being warehoused for a few years under the obsolete theory of "punishment," and then released back into society to commit more crimes (often more anti-social than ever after being "punished"), violent offenders will be subjected to (and benefit from) a fully-funded, serious effort to help them learn to live constructive lives in our society. (5) Finally, if a chief reason for increased prison sentences' current lack of deterrence is that criminals and prospective criminals don't know what the consequences of criminal acts will be (and/or feel that they may game the system into lower sentences) our system makes things very simple and clear. *Any* act of serious violence (what are today variously, and in various degrees, called murder, manslaughter, assault, aggravated assault, rape, child sexual abuse and etc.) will result in at least 5 years in a correctional facility, 20 years if the victim dies. Any *second* conviction for serious violence will result in life in prison. This is conceptually simple and will be both taught in public schools and widely publicized; so that anyone contemplating using violence against their fellow citizens will know precisely what the consequences will be if they are caught and convicted.

For the commission of less serious violent acts (those that cannot "reasonably be expected to risk lifelong impairment, including disfigurement, or death") the system of rehabilitative incarceration used for serious violent acts will be modified. In these cases, which will include everything from shoving or grabbing, to threats of violence, to a kick in the pants or slap in the face, first offenses will be dealt with through supervised probation, mandatory counseling and restitution to the victim. Repeat offenders, however, will be incarcerated in rehabilitative centers, though under terms different than those applied in cases of "serious" violent acts. First, sentences will be one year rather than ten; sentences will be fixed, rather than "to life"; and this group of offenders will not be housed in the same facilities as those guilty of serious violent acts. As in the case of crimes of serious violence, the invariable penalties for these less serious acts will be widely publicized. If we are to live in the just and humane society longed for by social democrats, it must be firmly established that acts of violence against one's fellow citizens *will not be tolerated.* In our social democratic future, every student at the end of elementary school will be aware that if you commit a violent act you will be dealt with very sternly; and if it is a serious violent act, you will be removed from society for *at least* 5 years (10 in the case of rape and child sexual abuse or if there are life-impairing injuries, 20 if the victim dies). No exceptions.

To move on to property crimes, while these do not generally inflict the same degree of harm on victims as violent crimes, they still do inflict harm (in the case of large thefts, a great deal) as well as feelings of violation upon victims. As already stated, we work hard to achieve the things we own, and to have them taken unjustly is painful and in some cases life-altering. It is the duty of the state to keep us secure in our possessions. Keeping with the principles already established in my discussion of violent crimes (that penalties must be clear and fixed in order to deter criminal activity) property crimes should also be met with clear penalties. Given that petty property crimes are far less damaging to victims than violent crimes, and far less disruptive to our daily lives, we will preserve incarceration in rehabilitative facilities only for the worst repeat offenders and those guilty of large-scale property crimes. We will dissuade small-scale theft by fines, supervised probation, counseling and an insistence upon restitution. If this cannot be achieved, rehabilitative incarceration would be the next step.

A Word on Policing

Our future social democratic America will invest whatever is necessary to keep its citizens safe. No child (or adult) should have to negotiate a neighborhood rife with violence, guns and unscrupulous gangsters pushing dangerous chemical substances. In dense urban areas we will reinstitute the beat cop, stationed at a climate-controlled kiosk and making regular rounds, on foot, throughout a territory that will cover something like nine square blocks (three blocks by three blocks). These officers will be in continuous communication with one another and their local station when backup is needed. Their proximity will be such that an alarm beacon, if activated by a local resident facing a threat of criminal behavior, will be heard by one or more officers, who will then rush to the scene. These officers will get to know the neighborhoods they work in and can fulfill a valuable community liason function along with their other duties. To get the greatest bang for the taxpayer dollar, they could provide other functions as well, such as code inspections.

Police, in our social democratic future, will embody the slogan "protect and serve." Police misconduct will be minimized by several measures.

First, we will require all officers to possess at minimum an associate degree with a major in criminology. Intensive study of the U.S. Constitution, and particularly the 4th Amendment, will be mandatory both on the college level and at police academies. Salaries for police officers will be sufficient to attract women and men with the proper aptitude, education and temperament for this vital but dangerous public service occupation.

Second, the Supreme Court must revert to the more stringent requirements for stop and frisk prevailing before the 1968 Supreme Court decision in *Ohio v Terry*. This decision altered the conditions necessary for police to detain and search persons from "probable cause" (there is a *better-than-even* chance that an individual has committed, is in the process of committing, or is about to commit a crime) with the far vaguer, and constitutionally unsupportable, "reasonable suspicion." The ruling has led to untold instances (in the hundreds of thousands in New York City alone) of harassment of law-abiding American citizens who, as Supreme Court Justice Louis Brandeis famously wrote, have the right "to be let alone."[7]

---

7. For a fuller treatment of *Terry*, see my article, "Terry v. Ohio, Stop and Frisk, and the Making of the American Police State" at

Third, each community (a city, ward of a city, a county) will have an elected police review board. These boards will hold regular hearings at which citizens can air complaints about improper police behavior; mechanisms will also exist to enable citizens to make such complaints behind closed doors. The boards will have both standing legal counsel and subpoena power and, vitally, the absolute authority to dismiss from public employment any police officer they deem, for any reason, unfit to serve in their communities.

Finally, the mere possession of psychoactive substances of any kind will cease to be a crime. States and the federal government will retain the authority to prosecute sellers of substances they deem harmful to their communities; but the victims of these pushers will be treated as a public health, not a criminal problem. This measure alone will greatly reduce interactions between police and citizens, thereby further reducing the chances of potential police abuse.[8]

"thesocialdemocrat.us."

8. Crime response in the U.S. is chiefly a state responsiblity, so establishing a system such as that described in this chapter will require action from 51 separate legislatures. This will be challenging, but physical and psychological safety being such a vital human need, it is my view that something resembling the systems I propose here will be crucial to creating the just and humane civilization this volume promotes.

Nuts & Bolts

Identity Group Claims

A key strain of the American Left today is the advancing of
identity group claims. As put forth in this volume's introduction, the advancing of identity group claims is *not* social democracy. That is not to say that a social democrat like myself is
insensitive to identity group claims—or that I dismiss their rel-
evance across the board, or that they could not play some part
in a social democratic polity—but merely that such claims are
not a necessary or essential feature of social democracy as a
system of social-political organization. Having said that, the
question yet remains, what role should identity group claims
play in America's social democratic future? In this chapter we
will first look at the claims of racialized identity groups; we will
then briefly consider the changing role of women in American society and the implications of our transition, already well
under way, to a gender-neutral workforce.

Racialized Identity Groups

Let's consider two possible approaches to racialized identity
group claims. On the one hand, one might envision a society where, as a fixed and permanent feature, citizens claim
identity with one among many racialized groups, and all government programs and policies are tailored separately to fit
each of the different groups. One set of rules, policies and
programs for Americans racialized as "Asian" (ARAs), another set for Americans racialized as "Black" (ARBs), another for
Americans racialized as "Native American" (ARNAs), another
for Americans racialized as "White" (ARWs), and so on. Establishing such a system on a permanent basis would imply a

belief that these racialized identities describe real, permanent and inalterable differences (this is what we might call the "essentializing" of the concept of race).

On the other hand, we can imagine a society where, in order to correct past injustices, some racialized groups are *temporarily* treated differently than others, while holding to the belief that our racialized identities do not describe any inalterable or essential differences, and that we are striving toward an ideal by which each *individual* receives equal treatment: a society in which, as Martin Luther King famously said, people are judged not by "the color of their skin" but by "the content of their character."

I think it can be safely said that the vast majority of Americans who believe in differing treatment for some racialized identity groups hold to the second of the two systems just described: that such disparate treatment is required to rectify past or even present injustices, and that its remit should be temporary, lasting only as long as it takes to make the injured party whole and/or until the present system is perceived as "just."

Chief among the racialized identity groups on whose behalf claims are advanced that they are entitled to special consideration due to past and/or present injustices (both by self-proclaimed spokespeople and by those outside the racialized group in question) are Americans racialized as "Black" (ARBs); Americans racialized as "Latino" (ARLs); Americans racialized as "Native American" (ARNAs); and Americans racialized as "Asian" (ARAs), though these are by no means the only ones. Self-designated spokespeople for these groups generally claim, in each of these cases, that their ancestors were treated unfairly in this nation (unequal treatment both before the law and from private citizens) and also that they continue to be treated unfairly, if not officially by the state then in myriad ways, some more subtle than others, by private citizens.

No person with even a passing familiarity with United States history can doubt that individuals racialized into each of the identity groups mentioned above have, in the past, suffered unequal treatment both by the United States government, state and municipal governments and by private parties. The extent and nature of any ongoing mistreatment of citizens identified with these groups in the present, however, is more controversial. Certainly every government in the nation, from the municipal to the federal level, prohibits discrimination against individuals based on perceived racial differences. The behavior of private parties is another matter, and while there are clearly racist attitudes among a substantial subset of the American citizenry, it is my perception that the large majority of present-day Americans prefer to take each of their fellow citizens as they find them, without regard to where their ancestors came from.

The question still remains as to what role racialized identity groups should play in America's social democratic future. First I will reject out of hand a system that eternalizes racialized identity groups, for the criteria upon which these groups are determined are among the most superficial of our characteristics as human beings, lumping groups of people together without regard to anything more essential than the shape of their noses or which shade of brown their skin is. This is un-human, meaning that it runs against a true understanding of ourselves as one human family, and inimical to progress toward a more ideal society. This leaves us with the second option, where we might choose to adopt different treatment for some racialized identity groups on a temporary basis only, in order to rectify past and/or present injustices. Let us now examine this strand more carefully.

The mother of racialized identity groups in the United States is Americans racialized as "Black" (ARBs). In terms of numbers, ARBs were until recently the most numerous racialized group in the nation after Americans racialized as "White" (ARW); they have been in North America essentially as long as ARWs; and the systematic mistreatment that people in this group suffered through slavery, Jim Crow and apartheid is in a class by itself. The issue of what special treatment, if any, Americans racialized as "Black" should now receive from government can be broken down into three questions: (1) What remedy, if any, is appropriate for *past* unfair treatment of people fitting into this group identity? (2) Do people fitting this group identity continue to experience unfair treatment? and (3) If so, what remedy is appropriate for *current* unfair treatment?[1]

I am going to begin with what I consider to be the simplest case conceptually: that of ARBs, still alive today, who suffered government-applied or government-sanctioned unequal treatment during their lifetimes. Consider an 80-year-old woman and man today, born in 1942 who, for the first 25 years of their lives were relegated by governments to inferior schools, barred from lucrative professions, kept out of universities, told to ride in the back of the bus, turned away from hotels, run out of upcoming suburban neighborhoods: in other words, denied full and equal participation in American life and thereby deprived, to varying degrees, of the opportunity to thrive economically, socially and culturally. This was all done with, if not the active participation of the state (as in the South) then with its tacit permission. When the U.S. Government promulgated the Civil Rights Act of 1964, the Voting Rights Act of 1967 and the Fair Housing Act of 1968, we might say that the federal government had made discrimination based on racialized identity illegal throughout the nation, and that the nation was no longer complicit in unfair treatment. I think we can safely say, however, that anyone born before 1968 was subjected, for at least part of their lives,

---

1. My treatment of race in this chapter is admittedly cursory. The subject has insinuated itself into almost every area of American life and is fraught with a plethora of claims and counter-claims, some legitimate and many specious. By and large, my remarks on ARBs can be applied to other racialized groups. I have treated the subject more thoroughly in an article on the Social Democrat website (thesocialdemocrat.us), "Our Tortured Discourse on Race."

to officially sanctioned unfair treatment.

Based on this logic, I believe that any American citizen born prior to 1968 and who lived in the United States at that time, and who was racialized as "Black," should be paid reparations by the United States government.[2] I think we can confidently assume that the unfair treatment these citizens were subjected to, as well as the yet more egregious unfair treatment imposed upon their parents and grandparents, presented an unmistakable handicap in the run for the American Dream. We will further assume that the extent to which the net worth and income level of an ARB born in these years differs from the median net worth and income of Americans racialized as "White" born in the same year is the result of the unfair treatment to which ARBs were subjected. As to payments, they will be on a sliding scale, depending on how long the recipient lived under the pre – Civil Rights apartheid regime. The fullest payment will go to those who had attained the age of 18 by 1968: these beneficiaries will receive, first, a lump sum bringing their net worth up to the median net worth of ARWs born the same year (if their net worth is lower than that amount). Second, their annual incomes will be supplemented by an amount equal to the difference between their income and the median income of ARWs born the same year if their income is lower than that median. Payments received by those who had not yet reached adulthood in 1968 will be reduced by a fixed percentage for every non-adult year lived after 1968, so that the amount received by a person who reached the age of 18 in

2. See discussion of racialized identities and terminology in the footnote to page 11: The DNA-revealed presence of African ancestry among a large percentage of people whose parents and grandparents were considered, and are themselves considered, "White," would render it nonsensical to use "African ancestry" as the criterion for compensation. This factor will certainly also complicate the application of any reparations scheme, as there will now be an incentive for those whose parents and grandparents "passed" for "White" to now emphasize their African ancestry in order to make a claim on reparations. All of this, of course, highlights the extent to which our racialized categories are constructs of culture and society.

1969 will be 1/18th less than the full amount, a person reaching the age of 18 in 1970's payment will be 2/18s less than the full amount, and so on until a person reaching the age of 18 in 1986 will receive no payment at all.

Aside from being the right thing to do, such a reparations plan, making restitution for indisputable unequal treatment, will go a long way toward eradicating differences in wealth and income between ARBs and ARWs when these citizens are statistically aggregated together as separate groups. Consider that the lump-sum net-worth payments and income supplements for every ARB born prior to 1986 will be based upon the median net worths and incomes of ARWs who are currently 37 years old and older, which includes American society's wealthiest cohort.

Certainly all of these thresholds and figures are arbitrary; but there is a moral imperative to do *something*, and there is no way to precisely determine the exact extent to which the exclusion of ARBs from full participation in American life prior to 1968 affected each of these unfortunate individuals.[3]

The reparations scheme just outlined would be considered the final reckoning for officially sanctioned discrimination prior to 1968: each recipient of reparations payments would be required, as a condition of payment, to sign an indemnification agreeing that the reparations amounts given are accepted as a full and final compensation for any wrongs inflicted upon them and/or their ancestors. More than a mere legalistic formality (indemnifications being a standard feature of all payments resulting from, for example, insurance claims), this document would also carry moral weight and, as

---

3. I find claims, advanced by some, for reparations for mistreatment, including slavery, inflicted upon ARBs who are no longer living to be unpersuasive. While slavery and 19th- and early 20th-century Jim Crow were certainly heinously unfair and cruel, I believe the chain of causation to the life chances of any currently living person is so remote as to be nugatory. That is, I do not believe the mere fact of having an ancestor who was enslaved 200 years ago materially affects the chances of anyone succeeding in American society today.

such, represent the turning of a page: the recognition that past wrongs have been righted and that the time for blaming, and claiming redress, is over. We will never build a well-functioning society with a racialized identity group consisting of 13% of the population making never-ending claims of wrongs unrighted and demanding redress. And this brings me to the second and third questions identified in the introduction to this section: (2) Do people fitting this racialized group identity (ARB) continue to experience unfair treatment? and (3) If yes, what remedy is appropriate for *current* unfair treatment?

First let me address the idea that *any* disparity in current outcomes on various measures of either success (income earned, representation in corporate C-Suites, etc.) or life difficulties (suffering poor health, going to prison) between ARWs and ARBs is *ipso facto* a result of *systemic* racism. This is the line taken by Ibram Kendi and other promoters of so-called "anti-racism." I roundly reject these claims.[4] It is mere common sense that effective parenting, along with personal aptitudes, motivation and effort, play a large role in an individual's life success. A system in which every disparity between racialized groups, in the aggregate, led to immediate payments to, or special treatment for, all members of groups with lower aggregate numbers, would remove much incentive from members of these groups to strive to achieve. The possibility of relative success or failure, depending upon one's choices and the effort applied, is life's greatest teacher, a feedback mechanism that keeps all of us who are subjected to life's hazards in a state of constant learning. Any system that assures any person success regardless of their choices, or without effort, short-circuits this critical human process and destroys all impetus toward excellence. Ibram Kendi et al would have us believe that every failure to succeed of an ARB is due to "systemic racism,"

---

4. For a detailed, statistic-supported disquisition on some concrete reasons ARBs lag ARWs and ARAs (Americans racialized as "Asian") on many success measures, see Heather MacDonald, *When Race Trumps Merit* (2023). MacDonald inhabits the other end of the political spectrum from me; but her facts on this topic are persuasive.

yet this same logic would seem to force us to conclude that Americans with Jewish ancestry, who in the aggregate have higher incomes than other Americans racialized as "White," or that Americans racialized as "Asian" (ARAs), who in the aggregate excel in prestigious college admissions, are somehow being "systemically" *favored* over other groups—including ARWs. Such a system would lead, presumably, to such absurd outcomes as non-Jewish Americans racialized as "White" being compensated to match the considerably better economic outcomes of ARWs *with* Jewish ancestry, or ARWs being given special points in college admissions to bring their rates of acceptance up to those of ARAs. (We won't do either of these things, of course, because it is utterly obvious that the greater economic success of Americans with Jewish ancestry, like the greater academic success of ARAs, is due to the distinct kinds of world views and behavior patterns transmitted to children in these ethno-racialized categories by their parents.) By the crazy logic of racialized proportionality, we would further have to conclude that the hugely disproportionate success of Americans racialized as "Black" in professional basketball and football is due to some nefarious preference granted to members of this group and insist that all starting lineups have at least 59% "ARW players (or 76% if we include Hispanics identifying as "White"). We all know this is insane. Asking all members of society to strive for excellence and to make a positive contribution is not "blaming the victim." Those who take pleasure in preaching that "systemic racism" presents an ongoing barrier to success for American children racialized as "Black" does these children a great disservice. To the extent these impressionable minds believe this patently false mythology, their motivation, self-confidence and energy for positive self-transformation are impaired. With minimally competent parenting, there is no reason a middle or high school student racialized as "Black," of any income class, cannot study hard in school and at home, learn as much as they are capable of learning, and achieve any position in American society—from skilled tradesperson to entrepreneur to doctor to president of the United States—to which their native abilities lend themselves. The economic success of tens of millions of Americans racialized as "Black" is the clear evidence of this (according to a recent analysis by the Brookings Institution, around 61% of ARBs are "middle-class," and there are more than one million ARB millionaires in the United States).[5]

A chapter of my own family history might be apposite here. My father, born in 1931, spent the first 11 years of his life moving from one low-rent dive to another in Washington, D.C., with a single mother typically one step ahead of creditors and two sisters, his father having abandoned the family when he was three years old. When he was 11 his mother, who worked irregularly as a private nurse, often leaving the children unattended for long periods, remarried: this time, unfortunately, to an alcoholic who chronically abused my father and his siblings. After an attempt at a chicken carry-out in the capital city failed, the stepfather bought a farm in the Maryland countryside and moved the family into a shack with neither electricity nor indoor plumbing (you read that right, they used an outhouse for necessities, oil lamps for lighting and a coal stove for heat). An attempt to raise

---

5. I think it virtually self-evident that current lower success rates on many measures for ARBs, in the aggregate, can to some extent be traced back to pre – Civil Rights Era impediments, and possibly to a well-intentioned but poorly thought-out income-support program (Aid for Families with Dependent Children) which many believe incentivized, when coupled with a dearth of good employment options for ARB men, single-parent (mother only) homes and intergenerational welfare dependency. The vital question for today however is how to build a social democratic society which gives all Americans an equal opportunity to participate in the economic, social, cultural and political life of their communities, states and nation; and I believe it is through the programs I have outlined in this volume—which include, vitally, reparation payments for those most directly affected by pre – Civil Rights Era discrimination—rather than through continuing to racialize Americans, that such a result is most likely to be achieved.

chickens also failed (botulism), and my father spent the next several years in dire poverty. Literally lacking shoes to wear to school, embarrassed by his poverty and sick of being beat up by his stepfather, he left school after the 10th grade and began to work at a Safeway grocery store. He then moved to a smaller, neighborhood grocery. Here his good attitude and determination to succeed gained the attention of a visiting food wholesaler and he was offered a gray-collar job in the wholesale food business. Meanwhile he had joined the National Guard and married my mother, and through the Guard and with my mother's help and encouragement achieved his GED. Fast-forwarding 50 years, he retired in 1998 as the major partner in a wholesale food business with 41 employees. He once described his formula for success to me in this way: "If the boss said he was going out, and asked me to sweep the front store while he was gone, after sweeping the front store I'd sweep the back store, the storage room floor and every other floor I could find. Then I'd dust the shelves and (you get the idea) . . ." With three sons soon rounding out the family, he worked for the food wholesaler during the day, emptied boxcars at a local grocery chain's warehouse several evenings a week and spent Saturdays at the National Guard barracks where, taking advantage of every opportunity to learn something new and gain a new certification, he rose from buck private to first lieutenant in ten years. It should not be hard to understand why, when my father hears someone say that a child living in conditions any of us would consider luxurious compared to his primitive boyhood shack (a climate-controlled home with running water and electricity, for example, with cell phones and special college scholarships on offer) can't possibly succeed in life because they don't have every possible advantage, he feels like his head is about to explode. Nor should it be hard to understand why he finds the excessive victimization mantra currently in vogue with the identity-claim Left off-putting: or why he votes Republican! Now, do I believe that an American racialized as "Black," born the same year as my father, and in similar circumstances, could have lived my father's story? No, I don't. The *real* systemic and systematic racism of that era would not have afforded him the same opportunities. Do I believe that a young American of today, racialized as "Black," can replicate my father's story, or something similar? Absolutely, if that young person follows the same path my father followed: take every opportunity on offer to increase knowledge and skills that will benefit your fellow citizens; be courteous to others and follow generally accepted rules of decorum; work as hard as you can; don't break the law, as being convicted of crime can seriously derail your life (the only law I'm aware of my father ever breaking was the speed limit); don't have children until you are married and ready to provide them a stable home. These are the age-old rules for economic and social success in America. The American Dream has never been only about having things, but also about working hard, and living smart, to achieve them.[6]

It is already unlawful in the United States, as it has been since the 1960s, for anyone, government or private citizen, to discriminate on the basis of perceived racialized categories (as well as, since more recently, gender, age and sexual orientation), and this will of course remain the strictest of rules in our social democratic future. As regards more subtle forms of discrimination, so-called "micro-aggressions," or the fact that another may look at you differently, or harbor prejudicial attitudes, there is only so much government can (or should) do, in a democracy, in policing citizens' minds. I think it is fair to say that almost everyone harbors some unfair assumptions about people in other racialized or ethnicized groups. Just as some Americans racialized as "White" harbor

---

6. Of course, when we implement the social democracy I advocate in this volume, with guaranteed work or training at a living wage for those willing to work; affordable pre-K through college; effective after-school centers, and so on, no child in America will suffer anything even remotely resembling my father's Depression-era poverty, nor even the far less severe but still troubling deprivation undergone by the least well nurtured children of today.

stereotyped, prejudicial attitudes about Americans racialized as "Black" or others, many Americans racialized as "Black" harbor stereotyped, prejudicial attitudes about ARWs, Americans of Jewish Ancestry or Americans racialized as "Asian," and etc. This is not to mention unfair attitudes towards the elderly, bald people, those with high body-mass indexes or "nerds." We all need to strive to see one another as unique, precious and cherished fellow human beings rather than as representatives of some "other" group, with all the stereotypes built in. But I emphatically do not believe that the path to that better place is through doubling down on racializing ourselves, for this approach *cannot help but* fortify the idea that human beings should be divided into separate groups based on superficial differences in appearance, an idea which itself provides *the very basis for developing and maintaining harmful stereotypes.* Only a shared goodwill, and a willingness to give our fellow human beings the benefit of the doubt—that they are, by and large, decent and positively disposed toward others—will overcome these tendencies.[7] Any attempt to demonize any group—whether it be Donald Trump suggesting that immigrants racialized as "Latino" are thieves and rapists, or Ibram Kendi et al suggesting that all or most Americans racialized as "White" harbor unkind intentions toward Americans racialized as "Black" and wish to see them suffer and fail (a claim that while at least partially true 70 years ago is not, from where I sit, true today)—is counterproductive.

What I propose here is the idea, perhaps radical to some,[8] that if we wish to end the tremendous harm that has been

7. Alexis DeToqueville, the French aristocrat famous for his account of a 19th Century visit to the United States, is said to have made the following statement: "The United States is great because its people are good; and if the people of the United States ever cease to be good, the United States will cease to be great."

8. In the U.S., that is. In France, where the concept of *universalism* (every French citizen stands equal before the law) goes back to the French Revolution, it is unconstitutional for the government to even collect data on the basis of "race," much less use "race" as a basis for public policy.

done, and continues to be done, by dividing people into racialized groupings, that we *stop dividing people into racialized groupings.*

To the extent that poverty, or relative poverty, plays a role in reducing the chances of children in any aggregated racialized group (including ARWs who, incidentally, make up more than twice the number of those living below the poverty line—about 14 million—than ARBs—about 7 million), our future social democratic society will do everything possible, as explained in the earlier chapter of this volume, "Nurturing the Young," to equalize the playing field. Unless the state begins to raise children, however, much of a child's success will still depend on parenting: on providing a stable, safe and nurturing home environment with plenty of intellectual, cultural and social enrichment; on instilling healthy work and study habits; on establishing a firm moral framework (including respect for society, its laws, and the rights of others)[9] and where possible on maintaining a stable, two-parent marriage, as statistics clearly and consistently show that children of two-parent homes fare better than those in one-parent households.[10] As noted, a future social democratic America will do everything possible to make up shortfalls in a child's home life, with mechanisms such as, for example, the heavily-resourced after-school centers described above. Still, effective and dedicated parenting cannot help but make a huge difference in a child's success. To the extent that low

9. One-third of all males racialized as "Black" have felony convictions as against only 13 percent of the overall male population; according to FBI statistics, ARBs commit all crime at double the rate of ARWs and violent crimes at *six to seven* times the rate of ARWs. (See https://journalistsresource.org/economics/felony-triple-prison-conviction-black/)

10 According to the Annie E. Casey Foundation, births to ARB unwed mothers in 2022 constituted 63% of all such births (MacDonald); the figure for ARWs was 24% (https://datacenter.aecf.org/data/tables/107-children-in-single-parent-families-by-race-and-ethnicity#detailed/1/any/false/1095,2048,1729,37,871,870,573,869,36,868/8223,4040,4039,2638,2597,4758,1353/432,431).

wages and unemployment make good parenting and stable marriages more difficult for those who suffer under such burdens, our future social democratic America will address these issues through its system of living wages through guaranteed employment-or-training. Finally, reparation payments, as described above, to all ARBs born before 1986 will bring significant resources to households of that racialized cohort.

The vision offered in this volume is one in which we create a society that is both just and humane; one in which, through the practice of "radical inclusion," we attempt to ensure that every child (however racialized by some) can thrive and every adult (however racialized by some) make a contribution for which they are fairly compensated and fully participate in all aspects of American life. I believe that continuing to divide Americans into racialized identity groups is not only morally wrong and conceptually incoherent, but also that it will prevent the kind of solidarity which the society I am propounding will rely upon. It may be advisable, until we can institute the targeted reparations described above, guaranteed work-or-training at living wages, universal pre-K and affordable college, comprehensive after-school centers and effective oversight of police, to continue to track the progress of ARBs (and other historically disfavored groups) as we work to overcome the sequelae of centuries of racist mistreatment. I am convinced, however, that one day, in our social democratic future, we will dispense with racialized identity groups and just call ourselves "Americans."

Women & the Transition to a Gender-Neutral Workforce

Two factors, converging in middle of the 20th Century, worked together to produce perhaps the most radical change in human life since the invention of agriculture. First, the application of electricity and energy derived from fossil fuels had transformed an economy that was formerly based upon brute human and animal muscle into one based largely on knowledge and the manipulation of machines, rendering obsolete a sexual division of labor—and political power—largely premised upon the greater physical strength of males. Second, the invention of the birth control pill in 1950 offered the possibility to transform not merely human society but the very nature of human life itself. Whereas the exigencies of nursing and infant care kept pre-modern women tied to the home, women could now reliably determine when and if they wished to become pregnant. As human culture is a response to the environment in which a human group lives, these two massive changes in the circumstances of living in the modern world were bound to alter American culture. And perhaps the most significant change in that culture has been the emancipation of women (and men) from earlier gender-determined roles. Chiefly, for our purposes, that would mean women's increasing participation in the paid work force, initially in selected occupations (nursing, teaching) and now in all fields of endeavor, including some of the most lucrative (women now make up a majority of both college graduates and law students, and about half of medical school students).[11]

Over 75% of women between the ages of 25 and 55 are in the paid workforce in the U.S. Many of these women are also moms. About 65% of women with children under six are in the workforce, and up to 77% with children between the ages of six and seventeen. Clearly, for reasons both of personal choice and economic necessity, the large majority of U.S. women in the prime of their lives are in the paid workforce.

There is a statistic frequently quoted by those claiming to speak for women's rights, and continually parroted by politicians and in the press, that American females make 70 cents (recently updated to 82 cents) for every dollar made by an American male. Paired with the slogan, "Equal pay for equal work!" the implication is that employers all over America have men and women doing the same job for which they are paying the women less than the men. This, unfortunately, is a great example of Mark Twain's wonderful quip: "There are

11. Harvard economist and Nobel laureate Claudia Goldin refers to this sea-change as the "grand gender convergence."

lies, there are damnable lies, and there are statistics." It is true that the sum *total* of all American women, *in the aggregate*, make 70, 78 or 82 percent (choose your year) of what *all* American men make, *in the aggregate*, according to Census Bureau figures. However, as the research of Harvard economist and Nobel laureate Claudia Goldin has demonstrated, the so-called "wage gap" among American men and women is almost entirely explained by two factors: women, in the aggregate, choose less lucrative professions than men; women, in the aggregate, work part time more than men, typically to accommodate childcare responsibilities. In Goldin's latest work she has emphasized that the key to equalizing earnings between men and women lies in making work more family friendly.[12]

Given what Goldin's research has shown, a key social democratic role in facilitating a gender-neutral workforce, as well as in closing the male-female wage gap, will be to make sure that quality child care is affordable for all families. For school-age children, the after-school centers already discussed will play this vital role. For families with children below school age, government will subsidize childcare, with the criterion that childcare expenses not exceed a fixed percentage of household income. It should be further noted that the transition to a shorter work week, discussed on page 57, will greatly facilitate childcare for working parents of school-age children. Paid family leave for new parents is another crucial support for working women and, as research clearly indicates the importance of parental bonding in an infant's first months, a good investment in the developmental needs of our future Americans.[13]

---

12. *Career and Family: Women's Century-Long Journey toward Equity*
13. Should it need stating, the ability of women to control their reproductive lives through access to both contraception and abortion services is of course fundamental to facilitating equality in a gender-neutral workforce.

America's Social Democratic Future: Afterword

You have now come to the end of this small volume, and I appreciate your time and attention. As noted in my introduction, this book is not intended as a set of finely tuned policy positions, ready for immediate application, though that is not to say I don't stand behind the ideas presented here.[1] It is merely that public policy doesn't occur in a vacuum but in the give and take of the political process, and no program or policy was ever fashioned that worked a charm straight out of the box. Major initiatives championed in this volume, such as the guaranteed employment or upskilling Hubs, could only be designed after much consultation with relevant stakeholders in local government, business, labor and academic communities, and continually tweaked after incremental roll-out based on real-world experience. To again take the Hubs as an example, I believe I have presented a tight moral case here why something like them must be part of our civilization if that civilization is to be a just and humane one, based upon solidarity and inclusion. In their practical application, myriad details would be up for negotiation. The same can be said for all other policy recommendations made in this volume.

As regards racialized identity groups, and particularly Americans racialized as "Black," I recognize that lingering mistrust, anger, cultural bunkering, what some have described as a sort of inter-generational trauma, sporadic incidents of blatant racism even today and the real-world sequelae of past mistreatment may make my vision of a non-racialized nation a distant aspiration. I even recognize the possibility that we humans may just be too simple-minded to refrain from classifying others on the basis of readily ascertainable, superficial criteria. But one can hope. The immediate application of a

1. As noted in my preface, Lane Kenworthy's stunningly comprehensive yet highly readable volume, *Social Democratic Capitalism*, is full of practical solutions, presently applicable, based upon a long career studying social democracy within the rigors of academe.

reparations program such as the one outlined in this volume would go a long way, I am certain, toward achieving a re-set; and when coupled with other social democratic programs aimed at radical inclusion, give all Americans, regardless of where their ancestors lived 300 years ago, a shared stake in a new kind of society.

I have no doubt that, should this book reach any number of readers, it will annoy and even enrage some, for different reasons and in different measure, on both the Left and the Right. Our political discourse has unfortunately degenerated into the simple act of deciding which team you favor and then, like high school students at the football game, cheering on your side while denouncing the opposition, without bothering with the niceties of who has made the better play in any given instance. Criticism of this sort does not particularly bother me, for I am convinced that only when we begin to get out of our echo chambers, escape the dualistic discourse and, based upon a carefully considered political philosophy of one's choice, take each issue on its merits will we begin to fashion the sane compromises which can unite a solid majority of this nation's citizens behind a common program. As for criticism of the more thoughtful sort, I hope to receive large amounts of it. This volume is intended to begin a discussion about a new Left vision for America's future, not end it.

I freely admit that some of my policy proposals, for instance those involving the collecting of all natural resources, including land, into the Commons, would spell immediate disaster if proposed by anyone running for political office today. (Perhaps the more saleable approximation of this idea that I mentioned— the taxation of real estate transfers at a rate designed to capture unearned appreciation of land—would have a better chance at receiving a hearing.) The same can be said of my proposal to end inheritance. I have merely carried the principles of justice, solidarity, inclusion and democracy to their logical conclusions: if we find the results shocking, it is because we have become inured to living in an unjust, fragmented, exploitative and undemocratic civilization. Will America be ready to create a truly just and humane society, based upon solidarity and inclusion, during this election cycle? No way. In ten years? Forget about it! One hundred years? Maybe. After all, just 60 years ago I attended an elementary school where children whose features belied African ancestors were not allowed; where the governors of Southern states turned fire hoses on people who only asked to be treated like everyone else; and where women were told that the only proper functions they might perform in our society were homemaker, teacher or nurse. How things have changed in just over a half-century! In any case, I believe that the creation of a civilization based upon the values of social democracy is the only worthy journey for us Americans, even if the destination be far off. Meanwhile we can hope that pragmatists and practical politicians will do everything possible in the present to bring us always closer to the desired goal.

W. E. Smith, February, 2024

Addendum, December, 2024

I have argued, in this volume, of the need for the American Left, as embodied by the Democratic Party, to formulate a coherent political program answering to the everyday desires of average working Americans for good jobs at living wages, world-class education and career development for children and youth, safe streets, a social safety net that throws no one under the bus, and truly representative democracy—all shorn of separate messaging for racialized and other identity groups and moderately progressive on divisive culture-war issues. I believe that the recent national balloting, in which Democrats lost control of all branches of the federal government, while hemorrhaging voter share among working-class voters of all demographic groupings, makes this argument more compelling than ever.

W. E. Smith